As soon as they got outside, Charles took Ruthie's hand.

"I'm sorry for what I did to you."

"You didn't do anything." She still didn't feel like looking at Charles, so she pointed to a row of marigolds. "My favorite colors are all the different shades of orange and yellow."

"They're very pretty, just like you." Charles turned her around so she couldn't avoid looking him in the eye. "You're not only pretty on the outside, you are a beautiful person on the inside. I should have never been so abrupt with you. I'm sorry."

Ruthie had to fight back the tears as she nodded.

"So why don't we try to start over and talk about our next date?"

His eyes were still filled with pain, but she could tell he truly wanted her to forgive him.

"Since we went to the circus last time, why don't we do something simple?" she said softly.

She loved the way the corners of his eyes crinkled when he smiled. "I would love that. Got any ideas?"

Debby Mayne is the author of more than sixty novels and novellas. She writes family and faith-based romances, cozy mysteries, and women's fiction. She has also written more than one thousand short stories and articles as well as dozens of devotions for busy women. She has worked as managing editor of a national health publication, product information writer for a TV retailer, creative writing instructor, and copy editor and proofreader for several book publishers. Debby runs a Southern lifestyle blog, *Southern Home Express*, where she shares cooking tips, recipes and Southern expressions. She and her husband live in North Carolina.

J L W

UNLIKELY MATCH

Debby Mayne

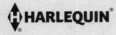 HARLEQUIN®

Recycling programs
for this product may
not exist in your area.

ISBN-13: 978-1-335-48500-7

Unlikely Match

First published in 2011 by Barbour Publishing.
This edition published in 2021.

Copyright © 2011 by Debby Mayne

This edition published by arrangement with Harlequin Books S.A.

For questions and comments about the quality of this book,
please contact us at CustomerService@Harlequin.com.

Harlequin Enterprises ULC
22 Adelaide St. West, 40th Floor
Toronto, Ontario M5H 4E3, Canada
www.Harlequin.com

Printed in U.S.A.

UNLIKELY MATCH

Chapter One

All Charles Polk had ever thought he wanted in life was to be a clown—a real clown with ridiculous makeup, baggy britches, oversize shoes, and an audience at the Ringling Bros. and Barnum and Bailey Circus. Then he'd started helping out on the Glick farm and realized he had a different calling.

"Ready, Charles?" Pop asked.

Charles stepped out into the hall of the house that had gone from being his parents' dream to their burden. "Ready."

All the way to the small Mennonite church in Pinecraft, the Polk family chattered about insignificant things to calm their unspoken fears. Even though he'd been there several times, his insides still churned with nerves.

Since most of the Mennonite families walked to church or rode their adult-sized tricycles they called bikes or three-wheelers, the Polk car was the only one in the parking lot. Charles knew his family was an enigma to the members of the church, but he prayed they'd eventually accept him without questions. Pop had assured him they would, but that was hard to imagine.

Charles walked into the church sanctuary with his parents, but Mom veered off toward where the women sat as he and Pop found a place among the men. There were so many things he needed to learn about the new life he wanted, but as the people who had come to talk to his family said, they had plenty of time.

Ruthie looked over toward the younger of the two new men in church and caught herself daydreaming about his past. She found it difficult to believe some of what she'd heard, but he did have an air of mystery.

Mother cut a glance at her and narrowed her eyes. Ruthie's cheeks flamed as she turned back to the pastor, who was right in the middle of his sermon.

An hour later, as she joined the other women getting ready for the monthly potluck, she overheard some of the talk about the Polk family. Ruthie's curiosity overcame her good sense, so she edged closer to the women doing all the talking. "I heard the boy was taking some classes to become a clown. Isn't that the silliest thing?" Sharon Bowles shook her head. "What kind of work is that for a man?"

"Perhaps that was a childish dream," Mrs. Penner said. "You know how children can be."

"None of our children ever dream of being clowns."

Shelley Burkholder Yoder scooted past with a casserole dish. "That's because they're already a bunch of clowns."

"Shelley!" Mrs. Burkholder shook her head and pretended to scowl as a smile played on her lips. "That is no way to talk about the fine young people in our community, especially since you're going to have one of your own soon."

Shelley glanced down at her growing abdomen. "Oh, I'm sure this child will fit right in with the rest of the clowns with a father like Jeremiah."

Mrs. Yoder chuckled. "My son might be a clown, but he's a smart one." She handed Ruthie a basket filled with biscuits and rolls. "Be a dear, Ruthie. Take these outside and put them on the end of the bread table."

Ruthie did as she was told, although she wished she could have remained in the church kitchen to hear what else the women had to say about the Polk family. As she walked past clusters of men, she sensed that all eyes were on the basket of bread she carried. Mennonite men sure did have big appetites. They never let more than a few seconds pass after the women gave them the go-ahead to pounce on the buffet line once the food was in place.

She glanced up in time to see Abe walking toward her. Her face burned, and her hands started shaking as they had since the time she acted out of character and boldly flirted with him before she realized he was in love with Mary. Although he wasn't interested in her in the least, he was still nice, so there was no reason for her to be so embarrassed whenever he came near.

"Hi, Ruthie," Abe said. "Looks like no one will go away hungry."

"Ya. There is always plenty of food."

"It's always nice to show off our hospitality to newcomers." Ruthie took a chance and met his gaze. "Ya." She knew his smile was meant to put her at ease, but she still felt like a bundle of nerves.

He nodded toward the Polk family. "Perhaps you can find some time to speak to Charles. He's a very interesting young man. Did you know he used to dream of being a clown?"

She looked down and tried to stifle a giggle. "So I've heard."

"I'm glad he came to his senses," Abe said. "Charles is a very hard worker just like his father."

Ruthie glanced toward the women who were hauling more food out to the picnic tables. "I'll try to speak to him, but now I need to help take out the food."

Abe took a step back. "Then I need to get out of your way. There are too many hungry men out here, and I don't want to be the cause of their starvation."

As Ruthie scooted past Abe and made her way back to the kitchen, she thought about Abe's warmth, kindness, and good humor. Those qualities were what had attracted her to him; she wondered if anyone else could even come close. She wished her older sister Amalie were here to advise her. Amalie and her husband had gone back to Tennessee to run his family's farm.

Mrs. Penner, Mary, and Shelley quickly gave her jobs to do, one right after the other, so she didn't have much time to think about her former attraction to Abe. But she did notice how many times the other women had her running past Charles Polk. Each time she looked at him, he had a different expression— all pleasant and very animated. He was attractive in an unconventional way, with reddish-brown hair that hung a little too long in front, deep blue eyes that were impossible to look away from, and a ruddy complexion from being outdoors in the sun.

"She's quiet but sweet," Jeremiah whispered. Charles pulled back. "Who?"

Jeremiah pointed toward the shy girl who stood slightly apart from the women. "Ruthie. I've known her since she started school several years behind me, and she's always been a tad shy."

There was never any doubt the people in the church loved to matchmake. As soon as the Polk family expressed an interest in exploring the Mennonite faith, he could tell that was one of the first things he'd have to face if they ever got serious about joining.

"Have you had a chance to talk to her yet?" Charles shrugged. "Just a few words. Not much."

Jeremiah laughed. "I'm beginning to think you're just as shy as she is."

"You know me better than that."

"Yeah, I know you from working on the farm, but this is different." Jeremiah's eyes twinkled as he leaned over and exaggerated a whisper. "This is about a girl, and they can be quite scary."

"No kidding." Charles glanced over toward the women again. Ruthie stood out with her chestnut-brown hair that was darker than most of the women's. Earlier he'd noticed her stunning blue-green eyes that were framed by long eyelashes. "She's pretty. I wonder why she's so shy."

"I get the whole looks thing, but do yourself a favor and don't make a big deal of her being pretty."

Charles cringed. He'd gotten so many things wrong that he thought he'd never fully understand how to act, even though it had seemed simple at first. "Is that not allowed in the Mennonite church?"

"Not that it's not allowed so much," Jeremiah said slowly, "more that it's not the place to put emphasis in your relationships." He chuckled. "I've always thought Shelley was the prettiest girl in town, and when I told her, she let me know there was much more to her than that."

"Thanks for the lesson." Charles appreciated Jeremiah's friendship. Between Jeremiah and Abe, he felt he had a chance of grasping the basic social aspects of being a Mennonite.

"Try to find some way to talk to her today." Jeremiah narrowed his eyes and folded his arms. "That is, if you're interested."

"I'm not sure yet." Although a handful of folks from the church wanted to matchmake, Charles had seen just as many skeptics. If any of them suspected he was even slightly interested in one of their girls, he was afraid they'd erect some sort of barrier to prevent him from getting to know her. He'd been reserved about expressing his opinions of Ruthie with Jeremiah, but he couldn't ignore the spark of attraction he felt whenever their gazes met.

After the women had all the serving tables loaded with food, Charles found his place with Pop. He lowered his head before the pastor said the blessing. As he raised his head and opened his eyes, he caught Ruthie staring at him, and his heart gave an unexpected leap.

"Go talk to her, son." Pop nudged him in the ribs.

"I'm not so sure this is a good time. Why don't we eat first?"

Pop opened his mouth, probably to argue, but he didn't have a chance before one of the older men approached and started talking. As the men exchanged words about farming, Charles mentally lectured himself about courage. He'd always been a little nervous about talking to people, which was one of the reasons being a clown had appealed to him.

Mom and Pop had taken him to a circus when he was in elementary school. He'd enjoyed watching the high-wire performers and the animals, but the acts that had intrigued him the most were the clowns. From a distance they seemed friendly, happy, and approachable, but when he got close, he realized that the makeup made them look that way, even when they frowned. And they didn't have to talk. Clowns were mesmerizing to all—from those who loved them to people who were afraid of them.

When his parents realized his obsession, they enrolled him in a clown camp sponsored by Ringling Bros. and Barnum and Bailey, where he learned some of the basics of making people laugh. He had fun, but something still seemed to be missing. After he graduated from high school, he enrolled at the Sarasota-Manatee campus of the University of South Florida and volunteered as a clown at the children's hospital. At first it was fun, but after a year's worth of performances, it started getting old. He wasn't sure what he wanted to do with his life, so he hadn't gotten past the general education classes in college. Then Pop asked if he was interested in working part-time at the Glick farm. By the end of the first week of repairing the barn, even after the rafter fell on him, he knew he'd found work that suited him. He'd never felt such a sense of satisfaction as what he experienced after working with his hands.

Ruthie couldn't stop stealing glances at Charles. At first he was engaged in conversation with some of the men, but as his father continued socializing, Charles had become withdrawn. He appeared to be deep in thought. She wondered what was on his mind.

"Go see if you can get him something," Shelley whispered. "Both of you are obviously shy, and someone has to make the first move."

"No one *has* to make a move at all."

"True." Shelley rested her hand on Ruthie's shoulder. "Why don't you take the approach of being friendly and showing your appreciation for his interest in being a Mennonite?"

"I could do that," Ruthie said. "But I still feel awkward."

"I'm sure he won't notice if you don't tell him. He'll just think you're a friendly girl who wants to welcome him."

Ruthie looked Shelley in the eye and nodded. "I'll go speak to him and ask if he's had enough dessert."

Shelley turned Ruthie around and gave her a gentle shove. "Then you best do it now before someone else does."

Ruthie took a deep breath and slowly headed toward Charles, her mind focused on putting one foot in front of the other rather than the fear that welled in her stomach. When she came within a couple of feet of him, she made eye contact and swallowed hard. "Would you like more dessert? There's plenty more over there."

A sense of numbness flooded her when he didn't immediately respond. Then a wide grin spread across his lips and he nodded. "I would love more dessert. Will you join me?" The next half hour went by so quickly it was more of a blur than a detailed memory. After she and Charles sat down with plates of pie, he asked questions and attentively listened to her answers. If she had any doubt about her attraction to Charles, it quickly dissolved. The last call for desserts went out, snagging their attention away from each other.

"I had fun, Ruthie," Charles said softly. "W-would you be interested in getting together sometime soon?"

"Ya, I would like that."

He stood up and looked down at her. "I'd like to make a date, but I'm not sure yet when I'll be available."

"I'll be in church next Sunday."

Charles smiled. "So will I. I'll talk to Abe and Pop then get back with you." He walked backward a couple of steps. "Good-bye, Ruthie. Have a nice week." Then he turned and hurried toward the parking lot.

"That wasn't so hard, was it?" Shelley asked from behind Ruthie.

"It was the hardest thing I've ever done in my life."

Shelley tilted her head back and laughed. "Trust me when I say there will be more difficult things to come." She put her arm around Ruthie and led her to the church. "So tell me all about it. Did he ask if he could see you again?"

Ruthie explained that he needed to check with Abe and his father before committing to a time. "I hope Mother doesn't mind."

"Why would she mind?" Shelley said. "Your parents are two of the kindest, most open people I know. They were both in favor of his family joining the church."

"Yes, I know, but when it comes to me and the people I associate with, they can be quite different."

"Trust me, I know how that is." Shelley glanced over her shoulder and spotted her mother staring at her. "Fortunately Jeremiah managed to win over both of my parents, but it wasn't easy for him or me."

Ruthie remembered hearing all about what Shelley and Jeremiah had gone through. "I don't even know Charles well enough to think that much into our...friendship. But he is very nice."

"Yes," Shelley agreed, nodding. "He's very nice, and he seems sincere about learning the Bible."

Ruthie helped clean the tables and church kitchen. After the remaining men put everything away, she walked the three blocks to the house where she lived with her parents. Mother and Papa had gone on a walk, so she had the house to herself. It was nice to have time to think.

"Ruthie Kauffman seems like such a sweet girl," Pop said as he maneuvered the car out of the church parking lot. "Have you thought about asking her out on a date?"

"I'd like to, Pop, but where do Mennonite people go on dates?"

His parents exchanged an amused look before his mother spoke. "Definitely not to a bar or dance club."

That was obvious. "Do you think she'd like to go to a circus?"

"I don't see why not," Pop said. "It seems harmless enough."

Mom's eyebrows were furrowed as she studied his face. "You're not still harboring the notion of being a clown, are you, Charles?"

"No, I've been over that for a while, but I still like them." He chewed on his bottom lip for a moment. "I just hope she's not afraid of clowns."

Pop stopped at the red light and winked at him in the rearview mirror. "If she is, you'll be there to protect her, just like I did when your mother and I had our first date."

Mom playfully swatted at Pop. "You took me to a scary movie just so I'd grab you."

Pop pretended to be hurt. "If we go through with becoming Mennonite, you can't keep beating me up."

Mom looked over her shoulder at Charles. "Now he's afraid of me. Go figure."

Charles was glad his parents' relationship didn't suffer after Pop lost his job of twenty years. The plummeting economy had caused his company to downsize, and he was part of a massive layoff. At first Pop had deluded himself into thinking he'd be in high demand, and it would only be a matter of time before some other company found out he was available and begged him to work for them. But that didn't happen. Pop and Charles both had to take odd jobs just to pay the bills, and there were times when the Polk family worried the power would be shut off. Mom worked, but her income didn't come close to covering the family's bills.

After they got home and settled in the house, Mom went to her room to change and Pop mentioned some of the work they'd be doing on the Glick farm during the next several weeks. "I never realized how much work went into citrus farming. After we swap out some of the citrus trees, we have to work on the irrigation system to make sure it's adequate for grapefruit."

"Do you think Abe will be able to give me more hours?" Charles asked. "I only have Tuesday and Thursday classes this semester, so I can work an extra day."

"I'll talk to him." Pop thought for a moment then amended his offer. "Why don't you ask him if he can give you more hours? If not, maybe Jeremiah can. He's talking about planting some summer crops. I suspect he would be happy to have another pair of hands."

Mom joined them. "One of you needs to cook dinner on Wednesday. I'm going over to Esther Kauffman's house for church instruction."

Charles gave Pop a curious look before turning back to Mom. "That's Ruthie's mom, right?"

She grinned. "Yes. Why?"

He shrugged a few seconds too late. "Just asking."

Pop laughed. "You'll be able to come home with some inside information on the girl. Maybe you can put in some good words for Charles."

"Jonathan," Mom said as she leveled Pop with one of her firm looks, "our son is perfectly capable of handling his own romance. He doesn't need help from a couple of meddling parents."

"After seeing some of the meddling among other people in the church, I think it might be good for Charles to have someone looking after his interests."

"I'm standing right here, Pop. You don't have to talk about me in the third person."

Pop lifted his eyebrows with a look of amusement. "Then stop acting as though you don't have a vested interest in your love life. Take action, son."

Charles opened his mouth to defend himself then thought better of it. Pop had enough on his mind already, between being behind on the mortgage payments and trying to make a decision about joining the Mennonite church.

Mondays were always busy for Ruthie. After a hectic Saturday and taking Sunday off, she had quite a bit of bookkeeping to catch up on. She generally spent most of the day in the office, so to get her out among people Papa occasionally had her work in Pinecraft Souvenirs, the family store, waiting on customers. Ruthie struggled with her shyness, and she found it difficult to talk to strangers. Fortunately most Mondays were slow.

Most of the customers were retired people—some were residents of Sarasota and others were on vacation. Ruthie didn't mind the grandmotherly types who shopped for their grandchildren. She stayed behind the counter and let them browse.

She'd barely finished lunch and had gone out to work in the store until the late-afternoon sales clerk arrived when a group of women from the church stopped by. She knew all of them except one— Charles's mother, Mrs. Polk, whom she'd seen in church a few times but hadn't spoken to yet.

"May I help you?" Ruthie asked in her quiet voice. She kept her attention focused on Mrs. Penner.

Mrs. Polk stepped toward her and smiled. "We just finished a Bible study, and they insisted we come here." The woman glanced over her shoulder at the other women. She smiled and whispered, "Now I know why."

Ruthie's lips twitched with nerves, but she managed a meager smile. "What are you looking for?"

Mrs. Burkholder glanced around and finally settled her gaze on Ruthie. "I'd like to pick something out for my grandkids."

The women began to nod and mumble their agreement. "That's an excellent idea, Melba," Mrs. Penner said. "How about those little chocolate alligators? I bet they'd like some of those."

As the women walked around the store, Ruthie caught them staring at her and whispering when they thought she wasn't looking. If Papa had been here, she would've run to the office and closed the door.

Finally a couple of them brought some small items to the cash register. After she rang them up, she noticed that Mrs. Polk was the last one out the door. Before she left, she turned, smiled at Ruthie, thanked her for being so patient, and winked.

Charles and his father went straight home after working on the Glick farm. Mom was waiting in the kitchen, so Pop said he'd tell her about his day before washing up. Charles took his time showering and dressing in fresh jeans and a T-shirt. When he came out to the kitchen, he heard his parents laughing.

"What's so funny?" he asked.

Pop looked back and forth between Charles and Mom. "Your mother's new friends are on a mission to make her a mother-in-law."

Charles sat down. "Oh yeah? Do I need to ask who the unlucky girl is?"

"Stop it, Charles. We're talking about that sweet little Ruthie," Mom explained. "After we finished our Bible lesson this morning, they asked me to stay for lunch. Since I'd taken a vacation day from work, I thought that sounded like an excellent idea. One thing led to another, and next thing I knew, we were going shopping."

Charles knew it had been a long time since Mom had gone shopping, even though it used to be one of her favorite pastimes. "Did you buy anything?"

"Of course not." She cast her gaze downward.

Pop laughed and gently nudged her. "Tell him what that shopping trip was really all about."

"We went to one of the little souvenir shops in Pinecraft," Mom said with a slight grin.

Charles raked his fingers through his hair. "What's the big deal about going to a souvenir shop?" His mind raced to find a connection.

"Tell him who you saw," urged Pop.

"Oh, that's right. Doesn't Ruthie Kauffman's family own a souvenir shop?"

"Yes," Mom said, "apparently so."

Chapter Two

"I heard you had some interesting visitors today," Mother said as she and Ruthie sat down for tea.

Ruthie looked down at the table, not wanting to look her mother in the eye. "Yes, some of the church ladies stopped by for souvenirs."

Mother laughed. "All this time living in Sarasota and suddenly they want souvenirs. Sarah Penner could have come up with something better than that."

"Business was slow today," Ruthie said to change the subject. "But Saturday's receipts were high."

"That's good," Mother said as she lifted her teacup to her lips. "What did you and the...church ladies talk about?"

Ruthie shrugged. "Not much. They were looking for things for their grandkids."

"I heard Lori Polk was with them."

"Ya." Ruthie set her cup in the saucer and leaned back, ready for the barrage of questions Mother would surely ask.

"She seems like a nice woman."

When no questions followed, Ruthie looked directly at her mother. "Very nice."

"Good. I'm happy we're attracting nice people to the fold. It would be difficult if someone with a bad disposition wanted to join our church." Mother stood up, carried her teacup and saucer to the sink, and turned around to face Ruthie. "If you want to see Charles outside of church, your father and I have decided we are okay with it, as long as you let us know everything."

That was such an unexpected comment that Ruthie nearly dropped her teacup. "I never asked to see Charles."

Mother smiled. "Not yet, but I suspect you will soon."

"I—I don't know what to say to him."

"Ruthie, I know how difficult it is for you to talk to people you don't know well—particularly men— but you need to get over that."

"I tried once with Abe," she reminded Mother. "And look how that turned out."

"Did it turn out bad?"

"He wasn't interested in me, remember?"

Mother sat back down, leaned toward Ruthie, and took her hands. "That doesn't make it bad. He was already interested in Mary at the time. You and Abe are friends now, right?"

Ruthie nodded. Yes, they were friends, but she still felt awkward around him.

"Don't let one setback determine your future. Remember that the Lord is always with you."

"I know that." Ruthie let go of Mother's hands and wrapped them around her teacup. "Maybe I'll talk to him next week at church."

Mother tightened her lips as she always did when she wasn't sure whether or not to say what was on her mind. Ruthie braced herself for whatever might come next.

"I hear he's talking about taking you to the circus." Ruthie's jaw dropped. "The circus? Why?"

Mother shrugged. "He told his father he might ask you to the circus. His father asked one of the men at the church if that would be acceptable."

"Why wouldn't it be?"

"I don't know. Perhaps he thinks there might be something the Mennonite faith would object to." Mother smiled. "I think it is very nice that he'd be so concerned. It shows his diligence and desire to do the right thing."

More than anything, it showed Ruthie another reason to be nervous around Charles Polk. She'd never been on a real date, and she'd never even had the desire to go to the circus, even though it was in Sarasota.

"Your papa thinks it would be a good place to go with Charles since you can go during the day and there will be plenty of people around."

Ruthie thought about it and agreed that going to the circus would be a safe date option—that is, if she ever went on a date with Charles.

* * *

Charles had classes on Tuesdays and Thursdays, so he got to sleep an extra hour on those days since he didn't have to report to the farm. At first he needed that extra hour after long days of manual labor. But he was used to it now. Sometimes it was difficult to stay in bed after getting into the habit of waking so early.

Mom had already gone to work, but she'd left a note on the counter letting him know his lunch was packed and in the refrigerator. He smiled as he grabbed it and dropped it into his backpack. When he first started packing his lunch, he missed the fast food he used to grab every day. Now he looked forward to a healthier meal—generally leftovers from dinner the night before.

That wasn't all that had changed in the Polk family. Until Pop lost his job, the family had three cars. It cost too much to maintain all of them, so they sold two of them and let Mom drive to work. Charles took the city bus to class. He and Pop got rides to the Glick farm with David, an acquaintance of Pop's and the man who told them about Abe needing workers. Charles never would have considered being without his own wheels in the past, but now that he didn't have them, he actually liked not having the burden. Cars were expensive to maintain, and it wasn't always easy finding a parking place. As long as the buses ran in Sarasota, he could get to just about any place he wanted to go in town.

Charles had a tough time concentrating on the

professor's lecture during economics class. His mind kept replaying his conversation with Ruthie Kauffman at church. He'd had a few dates in the past, but being the class clown had put him in the position of being more of a friend than a romantic interest in girls' minds. Even on his dates, the girls had expected him to make them laugh. As much as he once thought he'd enjoy performing, he was tired of it.

After lunch he had two more classes before heading back home. And since he'd agreed to work for Abe on Friday and Jeremiah on Saturday, he needed to get his studying out of the way.

Charles had to walk a quarter of a mile home from the bus stop. Both of his parents were still at work, so he took advantage of having the house to himself. The aroma of the stew Mom had started in the Crock-Pot this morning teased his taste buds. He rummaged through the nearly bare pantry until he found a forgotten box of crackers shoved to the far corner. He pulled one cracker out, nibbled a corner, and then tossed the box into the trash when he realized it was stale.

He put on a CD and cranked up the music before settling down at the kitchen table to study. It didn't take long until the shrill music grated his nerves. Strange how that happened after being in the midst of the calmness in the Mennonite church.

He'd barely closed his book when Mom called his cell phone. "I have to stop off at Publix on my way home. Need anything?"

"We're out of milk."

"It's on my list. Anything else?"

Charles wanted to tell her to bring home some junk food, and lots of it, but he knew how tight the budget was. "That's all. Dinner smells good, Mom."

"I hope the stew tastes good. I bought some cheap meat on sale, and I'm hoping the slow cooker will at least tenderize it."

"I'm sure it'll be just fine." Charles knew how much their financial situation had devastated his parents, but at least they were still together. He knew other couples in their situation who'd split when times got tough.

"Have you called Stan about getting circus tickets?"

"Not yet," Charles replied. "But I will soon."

"Don't wait too long. After he runs out of promotional tickets, that's it. Remember what happened last year?"

"Yes, I had to buy my tickets." That totally wasn't an option this year with money being so tight.

"I'm pulling into the Publix parking lot now. I won't be too long."

After Charles clicked Off, he thought about calling Stan Portfield, one of the clowns who'd worked with him at clown camp. The man had connections with Circus Sarasota and the Ringling Bros. and Barnum and Bailey troupes, so he could score tickets for almost any show. But as Mom had mentioned, there wasn't an unlimited supply.

He stood and started pacing as he scrolled through his phone list and found Stan's number then punched

Call. Stan answered with his standard "Wanna hear something funny?"

Charles and Stan chatted for a few minutes before Stan asked if he needed anything. "Do you have any Circus Sarasota tickets left for one of the shows at Ringling?"

"Of course I do. How many do you need?"

"Two." Charles paused before adding, "Is there any chance of getting a weekend show?"

"Yup, I have two weekend matinee tickets left. Meet me at our usual place tomorrow afternoon, and I'll buy you a cup of coffee."

"Um…" Charles hesitated before blurting, "I have to work tomorrow."

"I wanna give you these tickets, but you know how fast they go. I have lots of friends, and I can't very well tell them I don't have tickets when I do. First come, first serve, ya know."

"Yes, I know." Charles's shoulders sagged as he thought about his options. "Can we meet somewhere tonight?"

"Nope. I promised the hospital I'd be there for a kids' show. Wanna come? We can go out for pie and coffee afterward, like old times."

"Sorry, I can't."

"In that case, you better figure out a way to meet me tomorrow, or I can pretty much guarantee they'll be gone."

"Um… I'll try to meet you tomorrow afternoon. What time?"

"Are you out of class by two?"

"All my classes are on Tuesday and Thursday, so I should be able to make it at two."

"Good. See you then."

Charles punched Off then leaned against the wall and slid down to the floor. He sat there staring at the blank screen on his phone wondering what to do next. He knew how important responsibility was to Abe, but he didn't want to miss the opportunity to get free tickets to the circus.

The instant that thought flickered through his mind, he realized how ridiculous it was. The circus was fleeting while Abe's impression of him would last. Without standing up, he scrolled his list again and punched Stan's number. This time Stan didn't pick up. He didn't bother leaving a voice mail because he'd learned years ago that Stan never bothered checking messages. "If someone has something important to tell me, they'll call back," he'd said.

Charles tried Stan's number several times but to no avail. When his parents got home, they were so eager to talk about their days at work, they didn't even notice his silence until after dinner. He and Pop were putting away the food when he got the nerve to ask the question that had been bugging him.

"What do you think about me knocking off early tomorrow?" Charles asked.

"Is it for something important?"

"Not really." Charles thought for a few seconds then changed his mind. "Actually, it sort of is."

"I'm sure Abe will understand, but remember he

needs all the workers he can get, and you did commit to being there."

Charles explained his situation and how he really wanted to take Ruthie to the circus. Pop listened until he poured out all his thoughts.

"You done?" Pop asked.

"I've pretty much told you everything."

"Why do you have to go to the circus?"

Charles thought the answer to that was obvious. "It's all I know, Pop."

"C'mon, Charles. Give yourself more credit than that."

"I'm comfortable at the circus. I don't want to look like a nerd."

"There's nothing wrong with being a nerd."

Such a Pop thing to say. "Maybe not, but I'd rather get to know a girl in a place where I'm comfortable." He cleared his throat. "So do you think Abe will give me the afternoon off to get the tickets?"

Pop let out a chuckle of disbelief. "Ya know, son, I thought you had more integrity than that. You don't tell a man you'll work for him then back out just because something better comes along."

"But everyone wants me to take Ruthie out on a date, and you and Mom both said—"

"Sure, we thought it was a good idea for you to date a sweet Mennonite girl, but we didn't intend for you to go back on your responsibilities. If you leave early tomorrow, not only will Abe think less of you, but I'll be terribly disappointed in you."

"Stan said he has lots of people wanting those tickets, and it's first come—"

"So work to earn the money to buy your tickets. I don't see the problem."

"You know how expensive the good tickets are, Pop. If I have to buy them, I can't afford the decent sections."

Pop put the last bowl in the refrigerator, closed the door, and turned to face Charles. "Remember when we took you to your first circus?"

Charles nodded. "Of course I do. How can I forget?"

"Those were the cheapest tickets I could find. You were quite a bit younger then, so your mother didn't have a job outside the house. We barely made ends meet on my salary, but we found inexpensive ways to have fun as a family."

"Those were cheap tickets?" Charles asked. He reflected on that day and didn't remember sacrificing anything. "I thought they were the best in the house."

"Only because we made you think that. Now do the right thing and let Stan know you'll have to pass, unless he can hold those tickets until you're available."

Pop was right, but it sure didn't make things easy. He'd have to keep trying to get in touch with Stan, and then he'd need to set aside the money he'd make over the next several weeks to be able to afford two tickets to the circus. Even the cheap ones put a dent in the budget.

He finally got in touch with Stan the next morning as he rode to the Glick farm.

"I already told you I can't hold the tickets," Stan reminded him.

"Yes, I realize that. Thanks for offering them to me though."

"If you change your mind in the next few hours, call back." Charles clicked the Off button and turned to his dad. "You did the right thing, son. It's just a circus."

It was *just* a circus to Pop, but at least it was a place Charles felt comfortable and he'd have something to talk about. At the circus, he could point out some of the acts and explain some of the things the clowns were doing.

Friday and Saturday were grueling. Summer had begun, and the Florida sun beat down on the field, casting blazing rays on the workers' shoulders and necks. Charles didn't mind though. Now he knew what it was like to feel manly and worthwhile.

When Sunday morning rolled around, he was ready for a day off. Mom and Pop took their time getting ready, so Charles went outside and trimmed some of the shrubs while he waited. They finally let him know they were ready to go to church.

"Don't let Ruthie get away after the services are over," Mom said once they stepped inside the church. "Since you work and go to school all week, this might be your only opportunity to ask her out."

"I'll try, Mom."

She lifted an eyebrow. "Don't try. Just do it."

Charles laughed as Mom turned and headed for the other side of the church. All his life, Pop told him that trying wasn't always good enough when "doing" was what it took to get the job done.

Ruthie was about to leave the building after church when she heard her name being called. She spun around and saw Charles Polk walking briskly toward her. She reached up to tuck a stray strand of hair back under her kapp and licked her lips to keep them from feeling so dry.

"Hey, Ruthie, I was wondering if you'd like to… um…would you like to…" Charles had stopped about ten feet in front of her and had begun fidgeting with the paper in his hands.

"Would I like to what?" she asked when he didn't continue. "Circus Sarasota has their big summer event at Ringling Brothers and Barnum and Bailey, and I thought… Well, maybe…" He cleared his throat. "Would you like to go with me?"

Ruthie hoped he couldn't hear her heart pounding. "I've never been to the circus before."

"You'll love it. They have all kinds of fun acts. Even if you don't like one, there will be another one right afterward. I don't know anyone who doesn't like the circus."

"I guess that would be okay. When is it?"

"The end of June. I'll get the dates and let you know. Since I'm working and going to school, I thought a weekend afternoon would be best."

Since Ruthie's parents had already approved, she nodded. "I would like that."

He wiped his palms, one at a time on his pant leg, as he remained standing there. She wondered if he had anything else to say, but he obviously didn't when he said, "I'll be in touch. See ya."

How strange. Charles appeared just as uncomfortable around her as she was around him.

Even stranger was how the people in the church reacted when they found out Ruthie was going on a date with Charles. The matchmakers were delighted, but another group was so upset they stopped by to see the Kauffman family to find out if it was true. Howard and Julia Krahn led the group, followed by Daniel and Cynthia Hostetler and Clayton and Diane Sims.

"Look who's coming up the walk," Mother said. "And they don't look happy." She opened the door slowly.

Mr. Krahn had already taken the position of spokesperson. "We wanted to find out if the rumor is true. Is your daughter in a relationship with that Polk boy?"

Ruthie's face burned. Fortunately Mother spoke up. "All depends on what you call a relationship."

"You know what we're talking about. Are they dating?"

Mother opened the door wider. "Would you like to come inside and get out of the sun?"

"Mother," Ruthie whispered as Mr. Krahn turned

to consult the rest of the people in the group. "I'm not so sure that's a good idea."

"It'll be fine, honey. They just have a few questions that I'm sure I can answer very quickly."

Ruthie had her doubts, but she couldn't argue with Mother. All three couples marched into the tiny house with scowls on their faces.

"Have a seat," Mother said, gesturing toward the living room at the front of the house. "Or would you be more comfortable in the kitchen?"

"This is fine," Mr. Krahn said. "And this will only take a few minutes. We need to protect our young people from the wickedness in the world."

"I believe that is what the Lord would want you to do," Mother said. "Would you like some tea or coffee?"

The visitors exchanged glances before all shaking their heads. "Neh, we don't need refreshment," Mr. Krahn said.

The demeanor of the guests had softened, but now they looked uncomfortable standing in the small living room. Mother gestured toward the sofa. "Why don't you have a seat?"

"We can't stay," Mrs. Krahn said. "We just wanted to come by to remind you how important it is we protect our children's faith. Walking with the Lord is difficult in these times."

"Yes," Mother said, still smiling, "from what I remember, it always has been. We certainly appreciate your concern."

Ruthie remained standing at the edge of the room,

listening to everything. No one even bothered looking in her direction, even though they claimed to be there out of concern for her.

Mr. Krahn took a step toward the door, and the others followed. "Keep your daughter away from anyone who might cause her to stray," he advised before opening the front door and walking out.

"Thank you again," Mother called out as they filed out of the house.

After she shut the door behind the last of the group, Mother turned to Ruthie and shook her head. Her smile had faded, but she didn't look angry.

"Why do they hate the Polks?" Ruthie asked. "It's not like they're doing anything wrong. I would think they'd be happy to see another family wanting to know more about the Lord and the Mennonite life."

"I don't think they hate the Polks." Mother nudged Ruthie toward the kitchen. "They mean well. Unfortunately they're reacting to something they don't understand."

"What don't they understand?"

"The Polks' motives. Most of the naysayers in the church speak out of ignorance."

"Do you think the Polks have good motives?"

Mother sighed. "There's no way I can know for sure, but it appears they do. They seem to realize that the Lord has led them to the church by using adversity to get their attention."

Ruthie knew some of the details about how Mr. Polk had lost his job and how they were struggling to pay their bills. She admired them for turning to the Lord.

"Just remember, Ruthie, that when people say they don't want you associating with the Polk boy, they think they're protecting you."

Ruthie nodded. "I don't always know what to say."

"Why bother to say anything? They're going to believe what they want anyway, so putting up resistance will only fuel their argument."

Mother was the wisest person Ruthie knew. She never would have considered the ramifications of defending herself. "I have to admit something else," Mother added. "Your papa and I are concerned about you dating Charles, but we don't want you to turn your back on the Polks because we don't know them very well."

"If you don't want me dating him—"

Mother lifted her finger to shush Ruthie. "I didn't say that. All I'm saying is that you need to be cautious."

"I always am." Ruthie didn't mention again how the one time she wasn't careful had backfired.

Chapter Three

Charles woke up with a flutter of excitement in his belly. Three weeks had passed since Ruthie Kauffman had agreed to go to the circus with him, and she hadn't changed her mind. He'd seen her in church Sunday nearly a week ago, and she'd even smiled at him before looking away. Her shyness intrigued him.

He'd seen a change in Pop ever since they'd known Abe Glick. Even Mom had noticed it and said she liked how he'd taken his eyes off his own plight and concentrated on his spiritual life. She'd been trying to get him to go to church with her ever since Charles could remember, but he'd always found some excuse not to go. Charles doubted she expected Pop to embrace the Mennonite life so eagerly. Between being too tired and using bad weather as an excuse for not wanting to go anywhere, Pop had managed to attend church merely a handful of times each year. As a small child, Charles had gone to Sunday school, but as he got older, he'd become more like Pop. Mom had finally given up.

Charles had to laugh about Mom's reaction when Pop started talking about going to the Mennonite church. The only exposure she'd had was when they went to Penner's Restaurant in Pinecraft. Mom and Pop had always considered the Conservative Mennonites an oddity. After Pop started working for Abe, he mentioned wanting to check out the Mennonite church to see what it was all about. At first Mom had resisted until she got to know some of the women who showed her the advantages of living a simple life wrapped around a deeply committed faith. Now they wanted to be Mennonite. Life was *so* filled with irony.

When Charles asked Abe if he could have Saturday afternoon off to take Ruthie to the circus, Abe gave him the whole day. "I want you to be rested and in a good mood," Abe had said, "not worried about something you'll have to leave on the farm."

Pop had argued and said he thought it would be good for Charles to work all morning, but Abe's wisdom and position of authority overrode anything Pop had to say. Charles knew Pop had been humbled enough to not even flinch at Abe's direction.

"Charles!" Mom's voice echoed through the hallway leading to the bedrooms. He could hear her footsteps on the tile floor as she got closer. "I can't believe you're sleeping so late. It's almost nine o'clock."

Charles sat up in bed. "I've been awake for a while."

"What are you doing still in bed?"

"Thinking."

Mom folded her arms, leaned against the door frame, and smiled at him. "There's been a lot to think about lately."

He threw back the covers and sat up. Mom laughed. "One of these days you'll grow out of those things," she said, pointing to his Batman pajama bottoms.

"Not likely. These are adult mediums, and I happen to know they come in large and extra large." He chuckled. "Which I'll need if we keep eating at the church potlucks."

Mom pulled away from the door. "I need to leave in a few minutes. I baked some muffins, so have one of those and some fruit before you go."

"Thanks, Mom."

Charles thought about the changes in Mom as he stood up and started getting ready. She'd not only accepted the idea of learning about the Mennonite church, but she'd embraced some of their culture, including the desire to bake. Last time they went to one of the church's potlucks, Mom's goal was to make a dessert that would have people coming back for seconds.

When he got to the kitchen, he spotted the note Mom left beside the basket of muffins letting him know she'd left the car for him. Beside the note was a key. Times sure had changed for the Polk family.

He spent the rest of the morning eating, watching a little TV, and getting ready for his date to the circus matinee. His nerves were frayed. Charles had very little experience with women, and he sure hoped this date didn't turn out to be a disaster.

In spite of the fact that he'd learned to pray about whatever was bothering him, he couldn't stop the jittery nerves from taking over. The time finally came for him to leave. On his way out the door, he stopped and muttered a prayer. *Lord, I appreciate everything. Now please don't let me botch this date. You know how nerdy I can be.* He paused and chuckled. *Thanks for listening. Amen.*

On the way to Pinecraft, Charles listened to a variety of music, changing the station when something annoyed him. He eventually realized all of it grated his nerves, so he punched the Power button.

He pulled up in front of the Kauffman house and expected to have to walk to the door, talk to Ruthie's parents, and wait for her. Instead he'd barely gotten halfway up the sidewalk when she and her mother came out.

"Hi, Charles," Mrs. Kauffman said, a frown forming on her forehead. "Did you drive here?"

"Yes, ma'am." He smiled. "Mom left me the car so I could drive Ruthie and me to the circus."

Mrs. Kauffman glanced at Ruthie with a look of concern. "Are you okay with this, Ruthie? You can still change your mind."

Charles froze in his tracks. "Is there a problem?"

Both women stared at him for several seconds until Mrs. Kauffman spoke. "I didn't expect you to drive. Most of us…well, not many of our people…" She turned to Ruthie and then back to him. "Very few of the people in our church drive cars. We generally find other modes of transportation."

"Oh yeah, well, I guess we can take the bus or something, if that would make you feel better about—"

Ruthie stepped toward him. "No, I'd much rather go in the car." She glanced over her shoulder at her mother. "We'll be fine, Mother."

Charles helped Ruthie into the passenger seat and started around to the driver's side of the car before he stopped and turned to face Ruthie's mom. "I promise to be very careful, Mrs. Kauffman."

Her frown slowly faded, and she smiled and nodded. "Take good care of my daughter, Charles. She hasn't been on many dates."

Ruthie was so embarrassed she wanted to crawl beneath the seat. Why had Mother said so much? It wasn't any of Charles's business about how many dates she'd been on.

He got into the car, buckled his seat belt, and turned to face her. "Your mom is really sweet."

"She worries too much," Ruthie said. "I wish she'd learn to relax."

Charles laughed. "I say the same thing about my mom, but I think that's just what they do. It comes with the territory. I'm sure I'd be the same way if I had kids."

"But we're not kids… I mean, children. We're adults."

"Yeah, but this is our parents we're talking about. To them we'll always be children."

Ruthie thought about that and nodded. "I s'pose you're right. But it's hard to act like an adult when I'm constantly treated as a child."

Charles started the car and pulled away from the curb. "Isn't that the truth."

All the way to their destination, Charles talked about how much he enjoyed working for Abe. Ruthie felt her nerves calming as she learned more about him. To her delight, he was even nicer than she originally thought, but he still had some peculiar ways that puzzled her. Maybe if she got to know him better, she could ask questions. She didn't want to seem too nosy this early.

"So, you've never been to a circus, huh?" He stopped at a light, turned to her, and smiled.

She shook her head. "Never really had a desire to go."

"I think you'll enjoy it. There are so many different things to watch, I can't imagine not liking something about it." He counted on his fingers as he named some of the acts. "Besides the clowns, you have the high wire, trick gymnasts, the animals—"

Ruthie's eyes widened. "Does anyone ever get hurt?"

"Sometimes, but they practice enough to minimize that happening in front of the audience."

Ruthie couldn't imagine why people would put

their own lives in danger, strictly for the sake of entertaining a crowd. "I know you wanted to be a circus clown. Did you ever get a chance to perform at one of these events?"

"No, I never did. I enjoyed being a clown for a while, but after doing a few volunteer shows, I realized it's not all fun and games. It's a lot of work, too, and after the show's over, you still have to face the realities of life."

"Why would you think otherwise?" she asked.

Charles let out a good-natured laugh. "That is a very smart question, Ruthie—one I asked myself years after I let everyone know I planned to be a clown when I grew up."

"That's such an odd aspiration."

"Yes, but I've never been accused of being normal."

Ruthie couldn't help but laugh. Charles was absolutely delightful company. She reached up and patted the hair around her kapp to make sure it was all in place and properly tucked.

"I've been wondering something," Charles said. "Maybe you know the answer."

She lowered her hands to her lap and faced him. "What's the question?"

"Will I have to dress differently when I take the final step of becoming a Mennonite?"

"I don't know. I've never seen anyone do what you and your parents are doing." She cast her gaze downward. "It generally happens the other way, with

Mennonites going out into the world and not coming back."

They arrived at their destination. Charles parked the car and came around to help Ruthie out.

Ruthie looked around in amazement at the variety of people walking toward the huge building. "I've never seen anything like this," she said, her voice barely above a whisper. "Just wait until you get inside. This is nothing compared to the show."

As they approached the building, Ruthie noticed a few people staring at her. She was used to tourists stopping at the shop and acting as though she was some oddity to be gawked at. Now she was doubly uncomfortable because she was out of her element.

"Does it bother you to have all these people staring? If it does, I'll tell them to mind their own business."

"No! Don't do that. People always like to watch anything they haven't seen before." She tried to hide the fact that she was pleased he wanted to protect her.

His smile warmed her. "So you're saying it doesn't bother you?"

"I'm not saying that," she replied. "I just don't want to give people cause to think I'm a bad person."

"Why would people think that?" He tilted his head and studied her face, making her tingle all the way to her toes.

"I—I don't want to make anyone defensive. Let's keep walking or we'll never get there."

Ruthie was surprised at the electric shocks bolting up her arm when Charles took her hand and led her to the gate where he handed someone their tickets. Someone else gave them directions to their seats.

"I'm sorry I couldn't get better seats," Charles said as they sat down. "This was all I could afford."

"What are you talking about?" Ruthie pointed down to the ring in front of them. "We should be able to see everything from here."

He smiled at her and closed both of his hands around the one of hers he was still holding. "Thanks for saying that. Pop told me it wouldn't be an issue."

"What?" Ruthie had no idea what he was talking about.

"I'll tell you about it later. Right now I'd like to explain some of the things we're about to see." And he did, fascinating her with information she never dreamed existed.

Once the show started, Ruthie sat mesmerized by everything that happened, one act after another and some happening simultaneously. It was all so different and new she didn't have any idea what to ask.

Charles occasionally explained each act as it appeared, and it made slightly more sense. Then it was over. All the performers and some of the animals came out for a final bow.

"Well?" Charles turned and looked directly into her eyes. "What do you think?"

"I think…" She blinked, almost expecting everything to disappear as she woke up from the most confusing dream she'd ever had. "I think it's all fascinating and chaotic."

"That's the best description of the circus I've ever heard."

She pointed down toward a clown in the arena. "And you wanted to do what that man is doing?"

"Yeah, afraid so."

"But why?"

Charles shrugged as he stood and pulled Ruthie to her feet. "It's hard to explain. I've always felt as though my life was boring and no one would be interested in me the way I am. Clowns get quite a bit of attention, and they elicit reactions from people."

"They're funny, but in sort of a scary way."

"I know," Charles said. "And I liked that, too. No one really knows what to think about clowns because they do such unexpected things." He tugged her toward the aisle. "C'mon, let's get outta here. Want to stop somewhere for a snack?"

"Okay," Ruthie said.

She thought about Charles's comments about why he thought he wanted to be a clown. She understood more than he probably realized. All her life she'd felt invisible, but it never dawned on her to dress up in a silly outfit, slather pasty makeup all over her face, and throw herself around as she'd seen the clowns at the circus do. Even after seeing them, it still didn't appeal to her.

Ruthie had to shield her eyes against the late-afternoon sun as they walked outside.

"You okay?" Charles asked.

She nodded and was about to let him know her eyes were adjusting when a little boy pointed to her and asked the man beside him, "Daddy, why is that lady wearing that funny outfit? Was she in the circus?"

"No, but she should be."

Ruthie felt Charles's hand tense around hers as he pulled her toward the man and little boy. "We are not freaks. We are Mennonites."

The man snickered. "You just contradicted yourself. You religious fanatics are all a bunch of freaks if you ask me."

If Ruthie hadn't pulled Charles away, she wasn't sure what he would have done. "Come on, Charles. Ignore those people. They don't understand."

"I can't ignore them." Ruthie had managed to get him far enough away from the people, so she relaxed just a tad before he hollered back, "You need to find out what you're talking about before you teach your child a bunch of lies."

Ruthie wanted to crawl into a ditch and hide, but she couldn't. The man was heading toward Charles, his face colored with rage. "Don't you call me a liar, you—" She put her hands over her ears to block out the string of curse words that flew from his mouth.

Charles blinked and glanced back and forth between the man and Ruthie before looking the man in the eye. "Okay, calm down. I wasn't trying to call you a liar. I was just saying—"

"Is there trouble over here?"

Ruthie turned around and saw a couple of uniformed police officers. She started to say something, but Charles spoke up before she had a chance.

"No, sir. We were just trying to explain to that man and his child that we are Mennonites."

One of the officers offered a friendly nod. "I like you people. We rarely have any trouble from your neighborhood." Then he turned to the angry man and dropped his smile. "Would you like an escort to your vehicle?"

After Ruthie was fairly certain they were safe, she let out breath she'd been holding. She'd seen a few confrontations but never when her personal safety was in jeopardy.

"I am so sorry," Charles said once they were buckled in his car. "That man made me so mad I wanted to hurt him."

"Do you understand that once you become Mennonite you are not allowed to fight anymore?"

Charles gave her a goofy but apologetic grin. "That's what's so ironic about this whole situation. I've never been a fighter. In fact, the only time I was ever involved in a fight was when some kids decided to beat up on me one day after school."

"That's terrible!"

He shrugged. "It happens. Kids can be mean when they want to show off. Boys don't want anyone to think they're sissies. I guess that must be hard for you to understand—this whole thing about people being mean to each other."

"Oh, no, I do understand that. I've seen my share of meanness. Just because Mennonites aren't allowed to fight doesn't mean they don't find other ways to be mean."

"Well, I haven't seen it."

"Trust me," she said, "you will. That is, if you stick around awhile."

"So now where?"

Ruthie gave him a puzzled look. "Where?"

"Where would you like to go? Remember? We were talking about getting something to eat."

"Oh." She tapped her chin with her finger. "How about Penner's? They have the best pie in town."

"Sounds good to me. To Penner's we go!"

Ruthie tilted her head back and laughed. "You say the funniest things!"

He cast a quick glance at her before focusing back on the road. "You think I'm funny?"

"Very funny. I never know what to expect from you."

"And I thought I had to dress up like a clown to get a laugh."

Ruthie shook her head. "No, you don't have to dress up like anything other than what you are."

Silence fell between them, and Charles's expression changed from smiling to concern. "Does it bother you to think I'm funny?"

"Of course not," she replied. "I like to laugh."

"Whew. I was worried there for a second."

Ruthie laughed again. "See? That's what I'm talking about. You don't even have to try to be funny, but you are."

The rest of the way to Penner's they talked and laughed. Ruthie couldn't remember the last time she'd had so much fun and been so lighthearted.

They walked into Penner's Restaurant still laughing. Mr. Penner seated them at the corner booth where they had a view from two windows. Ruthie knew that was the best seat in the place. Mr. Penner gave her an understanding grin, making her face flame. She wanted to hide her face, but that would make her embarrassment obvious.

"So did you have fun?" Charles asked once they were alone. "I had a wonderful time!"

So Pop was right. Ruthie was perfectly content in the second cheapest seats in the house. She even said she thought they were in the best place because they had a good view of everything. In a way, she was right. They couldn't see all the performers' facial features, but they got a good bird's-eye view of everything.

He opened the menu and perused the different sections. The desserts weren't listed, but he could see a bunch of pies in the glass display case by the register.

A server approached their table and addressed Ruthie first. "Hey there, girl. How ya been?"

Ruthie smiled at the quirky girl in the apron holding the pencil and order pad. "Hi, Jocelyn. What kind of pie do you have today?"

"The best coconut cream pie you ever tasted. Want some?"

Ruthie nodded and looked at Charles. "Mrs. Penner makes all the pies, and I love her cream pies."

"Sounds good to me." He closed the menu and slid it toward the server.

"I've seen you in here before," the server said. "You got a name?"

Ruthie laughed. "Jocelyn, this is my...friend Charles."

Jocelyn arched one eyebrow as the corners of her mouth twitched into a grin. "Your friend, huh?" She looked directly at Charles. "Nice to meet you. You'll love the pie. It is totally delish."

After Jocelyn left the table, Charles gave Ruthie a questioning look. She leaned forward and spoke in a low voice. "Jocelyn started working here after Mary married Abe."

"Oh, that's right," Charles said. "I remember the story now."

"Jocelyn is different, but I've heard that the customers like her."

"And I suspect she's not Mennonite," Charles said. Ruthie giggled. "Whatever gave you that idea?"

"Something about the outfit, the hair, and all the makeup." He made a goofy face that had Ruthie laughing even harder.

"You should have seen her before she toned it down."

The bell on the door jingled, so Charles glanced up. "Isn't that Peter?"

"You know Peter?" Ruthie asked.

"I do, but only because of what happened to Shelley. I was at the feed store with Jeremiah once when Peter tried to start trouble. Jeremiah did a good job of diffusing the situation. I can't say I would have done the same thing."

"Yes, I know how Peter can be."

"He's not a very nice person, is he?"

Ruthie shook her head. "No, he's not, even if he is my cousin."

"Peter's your cousin?"

Her cheeks flamed. "Yes, his mother and my father are brother and sister."

"I never would have… I mean, you don't seem like…um…"

"That's okay. People are always surprised when they find out."

Chapter Four

A few minutes later, Jocelyn arrived with their plates of pie. "Here ya go. Enjoy!"

"Thank you," Charles said. "It looks delicious."

Ruthie appreciated how polite Charles always was. His manners had been impeccable all day.

After Jocelyn left to check on Peter, silence fell between Ruthie and Charles. If Ruthie had any idea what to say, she would have spoken, but most of the time words didn't come easily to her.

"I had a great time today," Charles finally said, breaking the silence.

Ruthie nodded. "Ya, it was very nice. How long will the circus be here?"

"Not long. They have two sets of performances every year—one in February and the other during the summer."

"Do you always go?"

"I try to see them at least once per season. The

man who spent the most time with me at clown camp still works with the troupe."

Ruthie sat up straight. "Was he there?"

"He's a behind-the-scenes guy. He used to perform as a clown, but something happened and now he helps produce the show." Charles paused before adding, "So I didn't see him."

"Oh." Ruthie didn't know what to talk about next, so she sat back.

Jocelyn stopped by their booth to check on them. "Anything else I can get you two?"

"I think we're fine," Charles said. He gestured toward Ruthie. "Unless you want something else."

"No thank you. I'm fine."

Jocelyn's eyes twinkled as she smiled. "I hope both of you have a wonderful day."

She turned toward Peter and hesitated before taking a step. Ruthie watched, waiting for Peter to act out.

"Would you like more tea?" Jocelyn asked, her voice slightly deeper than it had been seconds earlier.

Peter opened his mouth but closed it as he shook his head. Ruthie had never seen Peter hold back. He obviously realized Jocelyn wasn't easily bullied.

"Sometimes I wish I could be more like Jocelyn," Ruthie said after Jocelyn left.

"Why?"

Ruthie thought about what to say and decided she might as well be open with Charles. He'd find out eventually anyway. "It's very hard for me to speak my mind sometimes."

"Some people speak their minds too much," Charles said. "I find it refreshing to see self-restraint."

"You do?" She couldn't keep the surprise out of her voice. "Absolutely. Have you noticed that most people in their early twenties try to copy some of the crazy celebrities they see on TV?"

Ruthie looked down at the table, cleared her throat, and looked back at Charles. "I wouldn't know. I don't watch TV."

Charles slapped his palm on his forehead. "That's right. I forgot. I am so sorry."

"What is there to be sorry about? You didn't do anything wrong."

"There are a few things I'll need to get used to about living a simple life. I've been watching TV for as long as I can remember, so that's one habit that'll be hard to break."

After they finished their pie, Charles left a tip on the table and went to the counter to pay. Ruthie stood nearby, waiting and not knowing what to do, so she looked around the dining room. She felt awkward. Mr. Penner called out and asked if they were in a hurry because he needed to get something out of the oven. Charles said that was okay, he would wait.

When her gaze met Peter's, he smiled. Ruthie didn't trust Peter enough to think his smile was friendly, so she quickly looked away.

"Whatsamatter, Ruthie?" Peter called out. "Embarrassed to be seen in public with your new boyfriend?"

Enraged, Ruthie walked straight toward Peter and glared down at him. "You are the meanest person I know, Peter. Why don't you try to be nice at least once in your life?"

Peter burst into laughter. "Don't be so serious all the time, cousin."

"I don't like all your insults." Ruthie took a couple of deep breaths and tried to tamp back her anger. Even she was surprised by her action.

"It's hard to hear the truth, isn't it?"

"Are you this condescending to everyone?" Jocelyn said, startling Ruthie. She hadn't seen Jocelyn coming.

"What are you talking about?" Peter said. "This is a family conversation, in case you didn't notice, and last time I checked, you weren't in my family."

Jocelyn placed her hand on Ruthie's arm. "Want me to get Mr. Penner?"

Ruthie shook her head. "No thanks. Peter may be my cousin, but he's not worth the effort of pulling Mr. Penner away from whatever he's doing."

Peter yanked his napkin from his lap and stood, causing the chair to screech across the floor behind him. "You women are crazy. I don't have to put up with this."

"Sit back down, Peter," Ruthie said, her voice low and deeper than usual. "You're making a spectacle of yourself. I'd hate word to get back to your mother."

He glared at her for several seconds, causing Ruthie's pulse to accelerate. She had no idea what to do next. Charles had left the counter and walked toward them. "What's going on?"

Peter grabbed his napkin and sat back down. "Your girlfriend is acting crazy."

Jocelyn placed her hand on the table and leaned toward Peter. "Who's acting crazy?"

"You heard me," Peter said. "And she's not the only one."

As Peter and Jocelyn bantered, Ruthie saw something she hadn't noticed before. Sparks of attraction flew with the words. Ruthie turned to Charles, who had clearly noticed as well.

He placed his hand on hers and tugged her back toward the counter. "Stick with me, okay? I think they need to work through this on their own. Interference from us will just complicate things even more."

"I don't want to leave Jocelyn." Ruthie looked back at Jocelyn who remained in the same position, her face about a foot from Peter's, both of them showing off and trying to get the upper hand. "On second thought, I'm sure she'll be fine."

Mr. Penner approached the counter. "Sorry it took so long. I had to move a few things off the counter before I could…" He looked past Charles and Ruthie at Jocelyn and Peter. "What's going on over there?"

"Just a little spat of attraction," Charles said.

Ruthie gasped. She didn't think Mr. Penner needed to be concerned with this.

Mr. Penner laughed. "That has been going on for weeks. Peter comes in here with a chip on his shoulder, and Jocelyn keeps trying to knock it off. When he leaves, he says he's never coming back, and Jocelyn says that's a good thing because she doesn't want to see him again." He rubbed the back of his neck, still grinning. "But he always comes back to do it all over again. And Jocelyn is right there to argue with him. I don't understand why, but they both seem to enjoy arguing."

Charles paid, thanked Mr. Penner for the pie, and led Ruthie to the car. "I've known couples who thrive on conflict. It might sound like arguing to most people, but it's how some people show their affection."

"I don't think I'd like that," Ruthie said, hoping Charles wasn't one of those who did. She didn't think he was, but she still didn't know him all that well.

"I know I wouldn't," he said, putting her mind at ease a bit.

"Peter has always been rather strong willed," Ruthie explained. "He knows what he wants, and he stops at nothing to get it, even if it hurts other people."

"Yeah, I figured as much after he dumped Shelley when she thought he was going to propose." Charles pursed his lips and looked at her. "Sorry. I shouldn't talk about your cousin like that. It's bad form."

"That's okay," Ruthie said. "You didn't say anything I didn't already know. The whole family likes Shelley, and they were appalled by what happened. We all assumed she'd eventually be part of our family, but then Jeremiah came along."

"Jeremiah seems like a good guy."

"I think he is." Ruthie wasn't sure what all Charles

knew about Jeremiah's past—leaving the church and living a wild life before coming back. And she wasn't about to be the one to tell him.

They pulled out of the restaurant parking lot and headed toward Ruthie's house. She was content sitting in silence, watching the scenery as they rode.

Charles let go of the steering wheel with his right hand and placed it on top of hers. "Would you like to go out with me again sometime?"

She had to resist the urge to shout with joy, so she swallowed hard and nodded. "That would be very nice."

"Good. I'll need to figure out my schedule and see when I have some free time. Between school and work, I stay pretty busy. At least I know I'll see you at church."

"Have you decided to join?"

"My whole family is leaning in that direction. I have to admit I'm a little surprised. Pop wasn't much of a churchgoer. Even though Mom was, she enjoyed all the finer things money could buy. When Pop lost his job, I thought she might go ballistic and do something crazy like some of her friends did, but she didn't. In fact, she seems more at peace now than ever, even though we can barely make ends meet."

"When you said your mother's friends went crazy, what were you talking about?"

"One of them left her husband for another man, and another stopped talking to all her friends."

"That's terrible!"

Charles nodded. "I agree. It's a strong reminder

that people can't control every aspect of their lives, and when they refuse to give God the reins, things go from bad to worse."

"Sounds like your parents have a solid marriage," Ruthie said softly.

"Yes, and I eventually hope to have what they have." He pulled up in front of Ruthie's house. "Wait right here. I'll get your door."

Ruthie's family rented the small house in Pinecraft, and since it was already wired for electricity, they used it, although sparingly. The front drapes were open, so she could see a tiny spark of light coming from the back of the house.

"Would you like to come in?" Ruthie asked when they reached the front door.

"I better get home. This is the only car we have, and I suspect Mom is itching to get it back."

Ruthie didn't understand, but she nodded. "Thank you for everything, Charles. I'll see you at church tomorrow."

Charles felt a combination of elation and peace as he drove home. Mom and Pop would no doubt fire nonstop questions at him, and he was glad to have some time to gather his wits. He created some quick answers to satisfy them without having to explain some of the feelings he'd never experienced before.

Ruthie's shyness had obviously prevented her from quite a bit in her past, including getting into romantic relationships, which was just fine with him. He hadn't exactly been Mr. Smooth Guy. He chuckled to himself as he thought about how awkward he felt with girls in the past, yet with Ruthie he had more confidence than ever. That brought back something Pop had said about when he and Mom started dating. *"Your mother brought out something in me that I never even knew I possessed. That's one of the ways you'll know you're in love."*

Although Charles didn't know Ruthie well enough to say he was in love with her, he knew he loved being with her, and he wanted to get to know her better. What blew him away was that she said she'd like to go out with him again. The day couldn't have been better.

Mom and Pop didn't disappoint him. The second he walked into the house, they were both right there grinning, ready to pounce. He pretended not to notice as he walked by and hung the keys on the Peg-Board and headed to the living room, where he stopped and waited.

"Well?" Mom walked up right behind him, so when he turned around, they were face-to-face. "We want details."

"It was fun."

Mom made a growling sound, and Pop laughed as he approached. "You know what your mother is asking, Charles. Out with it."

"Let's see. We went to the circus and sat in the nosebleed section."

"Did that bother her?" Pop asked.

"Not at all. In fact, she said she thought we had the best seats because we could see everything."

"I told you." Pop appeared mighty pleased with himself. "So what else happened?"

"We watched the circus, and I explained some of what was happening when the clowns came out. After that we went to Penner's and had pie." He lifted his hands and let them fall to his sides. "That's about it."

"Charles." Mom tilted her head toward him and glared at him from beneath her eyebrows. "I know better than that."

"What else do you want to know?"

"Are you going out with her again?" Pop asked.

"I asked her if she wanted to, and she said that would be nice."

Mom and Pop exchanged a glance before both of them turned back to face Charles. "That's all?" Mom said.

Before he had a chance to answer, Pop winked. "Did you kiss her?"

Charles felt his face grow hot. "I didn't think it was appropriate. It seems awkward, ya know? I mean, she's been a Mennonite all her life, and…well, do Mennonite girls do that?"

Both of his parents burst into laughter. "Of course they do, Charles. They're still human."

"I just don't want to make any mistakes. I like Ruthie, and I think she likes me, too."

"Trust me, son," Pop said. "Ruthie is just as human as you are. If you make mistakes, she'll understand."

"Do you two need anything else?" Charles asked as he backed away from Mom and Pop.

Mom stood on tiptoe and gave him a hug. "We'll let you off the hook for now."

"Then I think I'll go to my room."

After he left his parents, Charles wandered slowly back to his room, unbuttoning his shirt on the way down the hall. He paused for a moment when he heard Mom's hushed voice; then he took a few steps back so he could hear her better.

"Do you think we should say something to him about our visitors this afternoon?" she asked.

"Nah, let's let him enjoy the aftermath of his date. I'm sure he'll find out soon enough that not everyone thinks he's good enough for Ruthie."

"I can't believe what they said."

Charles strained to hear the rest of the conversation, but they'd taken it into the kitchen, out of hearing range of the hallway to the bedrooms. Whatever the visitors said must have been bad for Pop to think it would ruin his date.

Ruthie stood staring at Mother, her mouth hanging open in shock. Papa's rage was evident in his bulging eyes and reddened face, but she knew he wasn't about to act on it.

"They actually said that?" Ruthie managed to ask in a squeaky voice. "Why do they think Charles is trying to use me? He's not that way. Besides, what about me would he use?"

"That's exactly what we thought," Mother said. "I

expected as much from the first group, but when the Atzingers and Conrads stopped by, your papa and I were at a loss for words."

"Speechless," Papa agreed. "I had no idea there would be so many concerns about outsiders wanting to join our church."

Ruthie felt an uncommon rage welling in her chest. "They didn't seem to mind them joining the church until now. Why would the fact that Charles and I are friends affect their opinions?"

Papa's scowl turned to contemplation. "They said they're trying to protect you, but I think there's more to it than that."

"What else could it be?" Mother asked.

"No telling. I think we should just tell people to mind their own business."

"No," Mother said, "that would only anger them. Why don't we invite the Polks over and perhaps get one or two of the other families to join us? That way we can show an example of Christian love."

Papa nodded. "We can do that, but you know we can't control what anyone says. The Polks might hear something upsetting."

"Then so be it. I'm sure they've heard upsetting words before."

Ruthie was still perplexed, and she felt an intense desire to keep anyone from hurting Charles's feelings. "I think that might be a huge mistake. What if they decide not to join the church just because some people are mean spirited?"

Mother and Papa looked at each other. "She has a point," Papa said.

"It's better for them to change their minds before they join than to join and become disenchanted."

Ruthie thought about that and agreed deep down, but now she had her feelings for Charles to consider. "Why don't we just invite the Polks over first and let them see how our family is? After they know that some of us are nice, we can include others."

Mother smiled. "Ya, that might be good."

"Why don't you talk to Lori tomorrow at church?" he said. "Ask if they'd like to come over for supper."

Ruthie didn't expect him to want to invite the Polks over so soon, but she thought that sounded good. She looked at Mother, who nodded. "Okay, I'll do that if it's okay with Ruthie."

"Ya, that's just fine with me."

Mother and Papa smiled. "Then that's what I'll do," Mother said. "Ruthie, why don't you and I bake some cookies right now so we'll have something to serve for dessert?"

They didn't discuss the visitors, but Ruthie couldn't stop thinking about them. When she saw them at church the next morning, she felt their disapproving gazes as they said their good mornings.

Mother spoke to Mrs. Polk who said she needed to consult her husband. By the time everyone left the church, arrangements had been made for the Polks to stop by for a light supper. Charles grinned at Ruthie. She knew her cheeks were flushed as she smiled back.

Chapter Five

Charles lay back on his bed, study Bible in hand. He wanted to spend some time immersed in the Word before going to the Kauffmans' house for dinner.

On the way home from church, Pop said he was uncomfortable about going because he thought they might have an ulterior motive—one other than simply getting to know each other. Mom told him he was being paranoid after a couple of people gave them the cold shoulder. Charles knew not everyone was in favor of letting his family in, but the Kauffmans were kind and open to giving his family a chance.

After a couple of hours, Charles's stomach started rumbling, so he left his room and went to the kitchen for a snack. The aroma of baked chocolate accosted him the second he entered. Mom was bent over the open oven, checking a pan of brownies.

"For me?" he asked. "I'm starving."

"No, not for you." Mom straightened. "They need

a few more minutes. I'm taking them to the Kauff-mans'."

"I thought they were having supper for us."

Mom rolled her eyes. "You know better than that, Charles. Never visit people empty handed."

"And since you're from Alabama, that means you'll come bearing food."

"That's right." She propped her elbow on the counter and tilted her head as she watched him open the refrigerator door. "There's some fresh pimento cheese. Why don't you make yourself a sandwich?"

"Mmm. Good idea." He pulled out the bowl of pimento cheese and carried it to the counter by the bread box to make his sandwich. "Has Pop lightened up about his suspicions?"

"No, but he has agreed that it's probably a good idea to go, even if there is an ulterior reason they invited us. At least we'll have a better idea once we do this."

"Sounds like you're a little skeptical, too."

Mom shrugged. "You have to admit, today was strange. Some of the people who were originally open and friendly basically ignored us."

"I wonder if it has anything to do with my dating Ruthie." He scooped a heaping mound of pimento cheese onto a slice of bread, spread it with a knife, and topped it off with another slice of bread. Then he lifted it to his mouth and took a bite. "This is good, Mom."

She smiled. "At least I still remember how to cook. It's hard to believe that this time last year we

barely had any meals together—we were so busy
with lives that pulled us apart. I actually thought it
would go on like that forever, and I thought I was
happy. But now I realize I was in a perpetual state
of numbness."

Charles put the sandwich on the plate so he could
put the pimento cheese back in the fridge. As he
worked, he thought about what Mom had said.

"I'm still surprised at my reaction when your dad
lost his job."

Charles put his plate on the table and sat down to
eat. "Why's that?"

She pursed her lips and stared down at the floor.
"I was relieved. I must have subconsciously known
that things weren't working for us before." She
looked back up at Charles with sadness in her eyes.
"We needed something to shake us up and bring us
back together as a family." Her voice cracked as she
added, "After your sister died…"

As her voice trailed off, Charles closed the distance between them and pulled Mom into his arms.
She shook as she sobbed for a few seconds before
pulling away. "Things will all work out," he said.

"Yes, I'm sure they will." She dabbed the corner
of her eye with the edge of her sleeve. "I can't help
but think that God saved us in the nick of time."

"What are you saying? We weren't exactly starving to death."

"Not in the physical sense, but I felt empty all the
time, and no amount of shopping ever filled me up."

"I didn't realize you were miserable."

Mom grinned with tightened lips. "I knew I wasn't happy, but until we were forced to come together and rely on the Lord, I didn't know how unhappy I was either."

"Are you happy now?"

"I suppose I am, but I'm still worried about things that I need to let go of."

"Are you talking about money?"

She nodded. "We still have to pay this crazy huge house payment. I don't know what we were thinking when we refinanced a couple years ago to make all those expensive updates. I hope we're able to sell soon and move into a smaller place."

"We can, but we'll have to get rid of a bunch of stuff. Giving up TV and some of the other things will be hard—at least for Pop and me."

"I'm working on your dad, but I think he'll come around soon. I think Abe's been talking to him, too. He came home a few nights ago and actually asked if we could have a quiet evening without TV."

That was a major deal. Until now, Pop had the TV on nonstop, even when he wasn't watching. He said the sound drowned out his worrisome thoughts.

Charles had heard his parents discuss the different church options, so he didn't have to ask why they'd chosen the Mennonite church. Pop admired Abe's simple life, and Mom saw it as a way to prevent them from falling back into their old pattern of acquiring more possessions. He understood that, but he didn't want them to regret any decisions.

After he finished his sandwich, Charles put his

plate in the dishwasher and turned to Mom. "What do you think we'll do at the Kauffmans'?"

Mom shrugged. "I understand that some of the families want to get to know us better, and I assume they're one of the first since you are dating Ruthie."

"Probably."

"You are okay with that, aren't you?"

"Of course," Charles said. "Why wouldn't I be?"

"You haven't exactly brought home a parade of girls in the past. I thought maybe you worried about your dad and me embarrassing you."

"No chance of that, Mom. I've always been proud of you. The reason I haven't brought home girls is I haven't exactly been a chick magnet."

Mom laughed. "They don't know what they're missing."

"I better go get cleaned up."

Mom looked him over and nodded. "Why don't you change shirts while you're at it? That one's pretty rumpled."

Ruthie kept looking out the window. The afternoon dragged, and she couldn't wait to see Charles. She was nervous about his family visiting, too, because she had no idea what the two very different sets of people would find to talk about.

"They'll be here soon."

Ruthie turned around and saw Mother standing behind her. "I know."

"He must be a very nice boy to have you acting like this."

"Charles is nice, but…" Ruthie paused to try to think of the right words. "He isn't like anyone I've ever known before."

"That can be a good thing, Ruthie." Mother took Ruthie by the hand and led her to the sofa, where they both sat.

"Did you know that my mother wasn't Mennonite when she met my father?"

"No." Ruthie remembered Grandma Abigail. "Why didn't you tell me before?"

Mother shrugged. "I guess I never saw a reason. My father was born into an Amish family. When his parents came down here, they eventually joined the Mennonite church. Mother was visiting the church with a woman who'd befriended my grandmother, and that's how they met."

"Was there ever any problem with that?" Ruthie asked.

"I'm sure there were plenty of problems in the beginning, but eventually people forgot. They were married forty years before Mother passed away."

Ruthie glanced out the window then back at Mother. "I wonder if Grandfather ever had reservations about her."

"If he did, he never told us," Mother said as she stood. "In fact, he said one of the things he loved most about Mother was how she could always see a different side of things. I knew she was different, but she loved the Lord as much as anyone."

"Yes, I remember." Grandmother was the person

who used to explain confusing passages to Ruthie when she first started reading her Bible.

"So your papa and I are open to you seeing Charles as long as we feel that he is sincere in his faith."

"Of course." Ruthie thought for a moment. "How will I know he's sincere?"

Mother smiled. "Pray about it and be open to the Lord's guidance. You should always do that anyway. Come on, Ruthie, let's put some finishing touches on supper. I want everything to be good for the Polk family."

They added cheese to the broccoli casserole, prepared a platter of fresh-cut vegetables, and set the table for six. Ruthie was thankful for something to do to settle her nerves. When they heard the knock at the door, Mother nodded toward Ruthie. "Want to get that, or would you prefer I greet them?"

"I'll go."

"Good. I'll be right behind you."

Ruthie opened the door to three smiling Polks. Mrs. Polk handed her a plate covered in plastic wrap. "Brownies."

"Thank you." Ruthie started to carry them to the kitchen, but Mother gestured toward the front room beside the front hallway.

"Why don't you have a seat in the living room? I'll go outside and get my husband."

Ruthie showed them the living room then carried the plate of brownies into the kitchen, where she left them on the counter. When she went back to join the Polks, they were just sitting there look-ing as awkward as she felt. For some reason, that made her relax.

"How long have you lived here, Ruthie?" Mrs. Polk asked.

"Most of my life. We came to Pinecraft from Pennsylvania."

Charles opened his mouth, but before he said any-thing, something behind Ruthie caught his eye. She glanced over her shoulder and saw Papa as he came toward them.

"Welcome, Polk family. We are happy you agreed to join us." He faced Mr. Polk. "Come on, Jonathan. I'd like to show you my shuffleboard court." Papa took a few steps before adding, "You can come, too, Charles, if you want to."

Charles nodded. "I'd love to see it." He smiled at Ruthie, leaned toward her, and whispered, "My mom is very excited about being here. She says you have one of the nicest families she's ever met."

Mother had already led Mrs. Polk to the kitchen, chattering the whole time. Ruthie could tell Mother liked Charles's mother based on her facial expres-sions. She felt her shoulders relax as she realized she was nervous for no reason.

Mrs. Polk quickly fell into conversation with Mother, discussing her lack of cooking during the past few years and how she'd gotten caught up in in-significant things. She said she was happy to focus on what was really important.

"I can see how that might happen," Mother said.

"I have to admit I've been curious about some of the things we don't have, so it's probably best not to indulge."

"You are so right." Mrs. Polk sniffed the air. "Something smells absolutely delicious."

Mother chuckled. "I hope it tastes as good as it smells. I really wanted to feed your family a good meal."

Mrs. Polk laughed along with Mother. "One thing I noticed at the potluck is how the women in the church like to feed everyone. I hope I can measure up."

"Trust me, Lori. No one is measuring how well you cook. We love to eat anything we don't have to cook."

A half hour later, the two families were seated around the table. Papa bowed his head and everyone else followed. After he said the blessing, he looked all three members of the Polk family in the eye as he spoke. "We are honored to have you at our table, and we hope you enjoy your time in our home. Now let's eat."

Everyone laughed and started passing serving bowls. Ruthie kept stealing glances at Charles, who seemed as enamored of her family as she was his. Mr. and Mrs. Polk were interesting and fun, and they seemed to have an excellent rapport with Mother and Papa.

"Do you have other children?" Mother asked Mrs. Polk. The instant she said that, Ruthie saw the distressed look Mr. and Mrs. Polk shared. Her stomach lurched.

Mr. Polk cleared his throat. "We had a daughter who was four years older than Charles. She was killed in a car accident when she was in high school."

"I am so sorry to hear that," Mother said. "We experienced the loss of a child, only he was much younger." Then she told about how the brother Ruthie never knew had drowned in a lake when the family was visiting some friends. "He was three years old and one of the most delightful children I'd ever seen. Our older daughter Amalie took it pretty hard. I never thought we'd be able to enjoy life again, but then Ruthie came along and showed us a whole new spectrum of light."

As the parents discussed their commonalities, Ruthie thought about how much sorrow both families had experienced, yet they still managed to go through each day, walking in faith.

She noticed that Charles was very quiet, so she lifted the basket of rolls. "Would you like some bread?"

He nodded and took the basket, but he didn't say a word as he broke open a roll and buttered it. Ruthie worried that something had changed between them.

Charles had been able to shove aside memories of his big sister Jennifer until times like this when his parents talked about her. He'd loved and adored her, and she never failed to be there for him. She was always such fun to be around, and she brought a steady stream of friends home. He'd developed crushes on more than one of them, although he never let any of them know.

He noticed Ruthie giving him concerned glances, but he didn't feel like talking now. She'd lost a brother, but that happened before she was born, so she'd never know or fully understand the pain he felt. The memory of losing Jennifer had removed all the joy of this visit.

Mom and Pop continued chatting with the Kauffmans, and they'd already moved on, although the conversation had become much more solemn. But still, Charles didn't understand how they could continue after bringing up Jennifer. "Would you like to see the flower garden Mother and I planted in the spring?" Ruthie asked. "We can go out there after dinner if you want."

"No, I don't think so."

Ruthie put her fork down, sat back in her chair, and stared at her food. He knew he'd snapped at her, but he couldn't help it. All Charles wanted to do was go home and be alone in his room.

Every now and then he noticed Pop giving him a stern glance, so Charles looked away. This continued throughout the remainder of dinner.

Finally, Mrs. Kauffman stood. "Ruthie and I can clean up. Why don't the rest of you go on into the living room? We can have dessert after our dinner settles."

Pop carried his plate to the sink. "I need to have a talk with my son anyway. We'll go outside for a few minutes." He darted a glance toward Mom. "Maybe you can help Esther and Ruthie in the kitchen."

She didn't hesitate to agree, but before she lifted a dish from the table, she shot Charles a warning glance. He knew he was about to get the riot act about his sullenness.

"C'mon, son." Pop started toward the door with Charles right behind him.

The instant Charles pulled the front door closed, Pop turned around, placed his hands on his hips, and shook his head. "What are you trying to do? Sabotage our new friendship?"

"No," Charles said as he looked down at the ground. "It's just that when Jennifer came up—"

"Jennifer is gone, son. I miss her as much as you do…maybe even more. She was our firstborn child, and from the moment I first saw her, she brightened every day. When she was killed, I felt as though the light had gone out and might never come back." He paused and looked Charles in the eye.

"That's how I felt, too. Still do."

"I know, and it's okay to still be sad over our loss." Pop raked his fingers through his hair and let out a shaky breath. "If I could bring her back, I would. You know that. But I can't. She's in heaven now, and we're still here."

Charles let Pop's words work in his mind, but his heart still ached. "I just wish you hadn't brought her up."

"It happens, son. And it will for the rest of our lives. When people ask us about our children, it's natural to bring her up. In this case, we learned that the Kauffmans also lost a child, so they understand what we've been through."

Charles couldn't deny that. "That must have been tough for them, too."

"No doubt it was, but they're still here, and they're living their lives." Pop took a deep breath and slowly let it out before looking back at Charles. "Do you realize that Jennifer told your mom that she loved the Lord and she wanted our whole family to start attending the church she went to with her friends?"

"I knew she was going to church, but I didn't know the details."

"You were awfully young, so you probably didn't understand what was going on, and we didn't like to talk about it much."

"I don't get why we didn't all go to church. Wouldn't it have made things better?"

"I was so angry about Jennifer dying that I refused to go, but your mother went, and she liked it. She said it brought her peace knowing this wasn't all we had to look forward to."

Charles remembered when the women in the church surrounded Mom and brought meals on days when she couldn't get out of bed. He didn't fully understand what was happening back then, but now it made sense.

"It took losing my job and working for Abe to realize the importance of faith in God," Pop continued. "And now look at me. I'm dragging you and your mother to the Mennonite church. Who would ever have thought?"

Charles nodded. "I can see the Lord's hand in this."

"So can I, son, and I think we need to remember that if the Lord can turn me around, he can certainly help us deal with the loss of Jennifer. She loved you, and she'd be the first to tell you to enjoy the rest of your life."

"You're right, Pop." Charles knew he still wouldn't be able to shake the sadness that had come over him during dinner, but he could at least keep reminding himself of what Pop just said.

"Why don't we go on back inside so the Kauffmans won't think we took off?"

Charles nodded. "I think I'd like to see the flower garden."

"Good idea."

Ruthie heard Charles and his father come back inside the house. She could tell Mrs. Polk heard them, too, because she stopped what she was doing for a second and a look of apprehension came over her. Mother was quick to place her hand on Mrs. Polk's arm and give her a gentle squeeze, just as she did when Ruthie was worried about something.

"We've been through quite a bit since Jennifer died," Mrs. Polk said softly. "It's been especially hard on Charles. Just when we think he's better, something sets him back. The sadness seems to stay with him awhile."

Mother gave Mrs. Polk a hug. "The sadness may always be with him. Sometimes I can't help but think about our little Hans and how he found joy in everything—from wiggly worms in the ground to the birds in the sky."

Mrs. Polk sighed. "I'm sorry you all had to go through that, but it's nice to know you understand."

"We do understand. If you ever need someone to talk to and pray with you, I'm always here."

Tears misted Mrs. Polk's eyes. Ruthie had to turn away to keep from crying over the pain she saw.

Charles appeared at the door and watched the women for a few minutes before clearing his throat. Ruthie knew he was there, but she couldn't face him after the way he'd snapped at her.

"Ruthie," he said as he took a step toward her. She looked up but didn't say anything.

"I'd love to see your garden. Would you mind showing it to me now?"

Ruthie glanced over her shoulder toward Mother, who nodded. "Good idea. Why don't the two of you look at the flowers, and when you come back inside, we can have some dessert?"

Chapter Six

As soon as they got outside, Charles took Ruthie's hand. "I'm sorry for what I did to you."

"You didn't do anything." She still didn't feel like looking at Charles, so she pointed to a row of marigolds. "My favorite colors are all the different shades of orange and yellow."

"They're very pretty, just like you." Charles turned her around so she couldn't avoid looking him in the eye. "You're not only pretty on the outside, you are a beautiful person on the inside. I should have never been so abrupt with you. I'm sorry."

Ruthie had to fight back the tears as she nodded. She didn't know why his apology brought this kind of emotion, and she certainly didn't want him to see her cry.

"So why don't we try to start over and talk about our next date?"

Now when Ruthie looked him in the eye she saw something different. His eyes were still filled with

pain, but she could tell he truly wanted her to forgive him.

"Since we went to the circus last time, why don't
we do something simple?" she said softly.

She loved the way the corners of his eyes crinkled
when he smiled. "I would love that. Got any ideas?"

"Well…" Ruthie thought about the different things
she did and realized it might seem boring to him.
"You might not think this is fun…" Her voice trailed
off as her cheeks heated up.

"You might be surprised. I'm not that hard to
please."

"We can walk on the beach or go on a picnic."

"I love both of those ideas," Charles said. "Why
don't we have a picnic on the beach? Nothing like a
little sand to add texture to the picnic food."

Ruthie laughed. "And seasoning."

"Now that we've settled that, tell me about your
flowers." He pointed to the periwinkles. "What are
those?"

Ruthie led him along the path as she pointed out
the varieties of flowers and told him what she knew
about them. "I'm sad that some of the flowers are
starting to wilt, but not all of them can take the hot
Florida summer sun, like these impatiens."

"If I tried to grow any of them, they'd wilt, even
in the best of conditions," Charles admitted. "I don't
exactly have a green thumb with flowers." He held up
his thumb. "But good thing I have a knack for vegetables and fruit. I don't think Abe would appreciate
my killing his crops."

She couldn't help but smile as he made a funny face. "Mother is the one who understands flowers. I used to overwater them. She's teaching me that giving any living thing more than it needs can ruin it."

"That's true with everything. Even people and animals." He touched the tip of his fingers, counting off the different farm duties as he named them.

"Do you see yourself staying in farming?"

He looked out over the yard, paused, and turned to face her, nodding. "There's always something that needs to be built or fixed, like a barn or piece of farm equipment. I enjoy being busy all day. Makes me feel like I'm doing something worthwhile."

"Do you think you'd like to have your own farm someday?" Charles shrugged. "I don't know yet. I'm still taking some college classes, but I'm losing interest in school very quickly. Mom and Pop used to push me to go to college, but now they're backing off."

"You know Abe went to college," Ruthie said.

"Yes, he graduated with a degree in business, which was a smart thing to do. From what I hear, he turned his family farm around from barely making ends meet to being a tremendous success."

Ruthie nodded. "That's what I hear, too." She wondered if he had any idea of the fool she'd made of herself when she threw herself at Abe. Ruthie decided to bring it out and get it off her mind. "I used to have a crush on Abe."

"You did?" Charles gave her a worried look. "What happened?"

Ruthie shrugged. "When I realized he wasn't interested, the only thing I felt was embarrassment. Since I wasn't all that brokenhearted, maybe I wasn't ready for a relationship."

"Are you ready now?"

"I don't know."

He smiled. "You'll know when it's time...at least so I've heard."

"Ready to go back inside?" The conversation had gotten uncomfortable, and Ruthie didn't want to stay on the same track.

When they walked into the house, their parents were already sitting around the table again, enjoying dessert. "Why didn't anyone let us know?" Charles asked.

"We didn't want to interrupt you." Mother hopped up from the table and grabbed a couple of plates. "Would you like coffee, tea, milk, or water?"

Ruthie and Charles joined their parents, who didn't waste any time resuming their conversation about the Polks' house. "It was Lori's dream house when we first bought it," Mr. Polk said.

Mrs. Polk nodded but looked wistful. "It started out being my dream house, but now that my dreams have changed, it's not so much anymore. If anything, it's become a burden."

"Then why do you hang on to it?" Papa asked.

Ruthie wished Papa wouldn't be so quick to ask that question. Everything was so simple to him— black and white with no shades of gray. But Ruthie knew most people weren't like Papa.

Mr. and Mrs. Polk looked at each other before she spoke up. "We've discussed it, but the housing market isn't all that great right now. Besides, where would we go? With my husband out of a job, we probably won't qualify for a mortgage on another house."

"Then rent," Papa said. "That's what we do, and we're perfectly happy."

"My wife... I mean, we never considered renting after we hopped onboard the mortgage train." Mr. Polk chuckled. "We assumed the market would continue to go up and equity would keep increasing."

"What does that matter if you feel that your house is a burden?" Papa asked. "The Lord doesn't want us to feel the burden from things on earth."

"Good point," Mr. Polk said. "That's something Lori and I should probably discuss...among many other things."

"Yes, think about it, discuss it, and do whatever you feel you need to do," Papa said. "Just don't allow your house to create a wedge between you and your faith. I wouldn't be able to sleep at night if I were in that position."

Mrs. Polk nodded. "We are having trouble sleeping." She gave her husband a contemplative glance. "Yes, I agree it's probably worth discussing. We can't continue as we have, worried about how we're going to come up with our mortgage payments to keep the bank from foreclosing. I wish we'd saved more money when Jonathan was working, but we never saw this coming."

"Even if you had saved money, it doesn't last forever," Papa said.

As the parents talked, Ruthie cast an occasional glance at Charles to see his reaction. He seemed to be taking it all in just as she had.

Mr. Polk finished his dessert and stood up. "We need to head home now. Thank you for everything, Esther and Samuel—the food, the conversation... and the advice. You've given us quite a bit to think about."

"We'll pray for you and that you make the right decision," Papa said. He turned to Charles. "I'm sure we'll be seeing more of you."

Ruthie cringed. Papa's assumption embarrassed her, but at least she knew Charles wanted to see her again, so it could have been worse.

They'd barely pulled away from the curb when Mom started talking about the evening. "I've never seen you so talkative, Jonathan. You've always been such a private person—particularly when it comes to finances."

Pop nodded. "I know. The Kauffmans are easy to talk to though. They don't seem judgmental."

"I can't believe I'm saying this, but I want what they have." Mom turned and looked out the window before continuing. "Outwardly they appear to have very little, but when it comes to the important things, they're richer than anyone I've ever known in the past."

Again, Pop nodded. "I agree."

"We should probably put the house on the market soon."

They pulled up to a red light and stopped. Pop turned to Mom. "We don't need to act on emotion. Let's think about it for a few days then discuss it."

"Okay, but I'm pretty sure I'll say the same thing then." Charles looked out his window in the back of the sedan.

During the past several months, his family had gone through more changes than they had in all the years before, and his parents still seemed to have a strong marriage. He had to admit that he missed having his own wheels, but he'd adjusted and discovered the joy of eliminating unnecessary junk from his life.

But the house? This was the house he came home to right after he was born, so he didn't know what it would be like to live any other place. His room had undergone many transformations, but it was still the same room, with the same window overlooking the backyard he used to play in as a kid.

Until recently, Charles couldn't have imagined his parents even considering moving anywhere, let alone to a rental house. The thought of them joining the Pinecraft community still seemed like a stretch. Those houses were tiny enough to fit at least two, maybe three, of them in their house.

All three of them rode the rest of the way home in silence until they pulled into the driveway. "I have to run to the grocery store," Mom said. "So why don't you leave the car out?"

Mom took off a few minutes later, leaving Charles and Pop in the family room. Instead of turning on the television as he normally did, Pop turned to Charles. "Want to talk about tonight?"

Charles thought for a moment then shook his head. "Not really. I don't have much to say."

Pop smiled. "Yeah, we've pretty much said all we can for now, haven't we?" He reached for a magazine on the end table.

Charles left Pop and went up to his room to study his lecture notes, but his heart wasn't in the lessons. He had too many other things to think about.

An hour later Charles heard the sound of Mom pulling into the garage. He didn't have to be asked to help unload the car. He was out the door before she got out of the car.

Once all the bags were inside, Charles helped her put everything away. He lifted the butter out of a bag and studied it. "When was the last time you bought real butter?"

Mom smiled. "I can't remember. All I know is that food tastes much better with real butter, even though it does have way more calories than I should have." She put an armload of things into the pantry. "I've noticed that the Mennonite women don't even mention diets or calories, and most of them seem perfectly healthy."

"Remember they walk or ride those three-wheelers they call bikes, so they're working off the calories."

"True." She shoved a couple of cans into the pantry and closed the door. "I think downsizing our house and belongings will have a positive effect on us."

"It already has."

"We still have too much. Even if we choose not to give up TV, why do we need one in every bedroom?"

Charles pointed to the one attached beneath a kitchen cabinet. "When was the last time you watched that one?"

Mom poured herself a glass of water and leaned against the counter to drink it. "It seemed like a good idea when I had it installed."

Charles laughed. "I remember you saying you could watch the Food Network and cook along with your favorite chefs."

"Who has the time?" Mom finished her water and put the glass in the dishwasher before turning back to face Charles. "And that leads me to something else. Today wasn't the first time your dad and I have talked about putting the house on the market."

"So when do you think you'll do it?" Charles waited for that sick feeling in the pit of his stomach to return, but this time it didn't.

"Soon. We need to get it ready to show."

"I'll help."

"Good. We'll need to get rid of the clutter in the closets and paint. That should help make it more presentable."

"If you want me to, I can trim all the shrubs back along the front of the house," Charles offered. "I might even ask Ruthie for advice on planting some flowers."

Mom smiled. "That'll be a nice touch."

They chatted for a half hour about some of the things they could do to make the house more attractive to prospective buyers before Pop joined them. "If you fix this place up too much, we won't want to move." Pop walked up to Mom and put his arm around her waist. "We need to stay in prayer throughout this process."

"That goes without saying," Mom agreed. "And we don't need to let up afterward. I have no doubt this will be difficult on some levels, but as long as we lean on the Lord, those difficulties will be overshadowed by the blessing of doing His will."

Charles couldn't move; he was fascinated by his parents' unity in this decision. They'd always gotten along, with the exception of a short time after Jennifer's death, but this decision was clearly the most bonding experience he'd ever witnessed. Even though he'd had a sliver of doubt about his parents being able to give up so many of their worldly possessions before now, he was certain of their convictions at this moment.

"C'mere, son," Pop said, motioning Charles to join them. Mom pulled him closer. "Group hug."

Pop chuckled as they huddled together. "I have a feeling we'll be doing quite a bit of this in the days to come. It's not gonna be easy, ya know."

"Of course it won't, and that's what'll make the experience even better," Mom said. "Working hard as a family to make this become a reality will help us as long as we're all on the same page."

Pop dropped a kiss on Mom's head. "I've been blessed."

"Do you think they'll go through with it?" Papa asked Mother the next morning during breakfast.

Ruthie sat at the table and sipped her coffee as her parents discussed the Polk family. She'd wondered the same thing.

Being without many of the possessions most outsiders had was never a problem for her, but she suspected it would be difficult to give up some of what they called conveniences.

Mother lifted one shoulder in a half shrug as she stood to get more coffee. "We can only pray for them and hope that the Lord keeps them on the path of His desires."

"Do you ever want anything we don't have, Esther?"

"Why would I?" she replied as she sat back down. "I have everything I need and want right here at the table." She smiled at Ruthie.

"How about an automobile or a television?" Papa asked. "Or a dishwasher or microwave oven?"

Mother's eyes widened playfully. "Can you imagine me behind the wheel of an automobile? I can barely steer the bike you bought me."

Ruthie chimed in. "Sometimes I think a television would be fun."

Mother and Papa both snapped around to face

her. Papa nodded. "I imagine a little bit of television would be fun, but from what I hear, it becomes an addiction that's hard to break."

"Anything can become an addiction," Ruthie said. "But we're so busy I can't imagine when we'd fit it in anyway, so we're just as well off without it."

Papa's eyes sparkled as he nodded. "You are so right, Ruthie. We are very well off, and we need to always remember that." He stood and pushed his chair back. "I better get moving. I've got more than enough to do today."

As soon as Papa left, Mother and Ruthie cleared the breakfast dishes. As they worked, they chatted about what they had to do all week.

"Papa wanted me to come in early to finish posting the weekend's receipts before the new girl starts," Ruthie said. "I don't understand why he wants me to train someone to do what I've been doing since I was a teenager."

"He wants a backup, just in case you're not able to work," Mother reminded her. "We've also been talking about how to help you overcome your shyness."

"I don't need someone else working in the store to help me with that." She tried to hide the fact that her feelings were hurt. "I'll work on it, I promise."

Mother smiled and patted her arm. "It's time for you to experience more things, Ruthie. We understand your not wanting to have a rumspringa, but you do need to prepare for life as an adult. You never know what surprises the Lord might have in store for us."

Ruthie assumed Mother was talking about the possibility of Ruthie eventually getting married and deciding to stop working outside the home. But there would be plenty of time if and when that ever happened. She didn't say anything, though, because Mother had already started talking about her Bible group.

An hour later Ruthie was in the store's office, lining up the numbers and making sure they balanced with the actual cash receipts. Since business was generally slow on Monday mornings, Papa walked around the store checking to see what they needed to order. Rosemary, the new girl Papa had hired, wasn't due in until right before lunch. He wanted to spend some time with her showing her around before Ruthie was supposed to take her to lunch at Penner's.

Papa had informed her that he was hiring Rosemary sight unseen, simply because he trusted Rosemary's aunt and uncle who'd agreed to let her stay with them when she first moved to Florida. She was from Ohio, and she didn't know anyone outside her family, so they'd hoped she could become acclimated by working and getting to know the Kauffman family. She and Ruthie were the same age.

Satisfied with how quickly the numbers balanced, Ruthie underlined the totals. She glanced up and saw Papa watching her. "How long have you been standing there?"

He grinned. "Long enough. Rosemary should be here any minute."

Ruthie stood and stretched her arms over her head. "I've been sitting in one place too long."

"Then would you mind taking over out here while I run to the bank?" He lifted his bank bag and waved it around.

"Of course I don't mind." The store rarely got busy on weekday mornings, and sometimes they didn't have a single customer during the ten minutes it took Papa to walk the block and a half to the bank, hand the deposit bag to the teller, and walk back.

"If Rosemary gets here early, show her around the store." With that he left.

Papa wasn't back as quickly as usual, so Ruthie assumed he either got sidetracked by a friend who wanted to chat or he wanted to be away when Rosemary arrived. He'd been commenting lately about how Ruthie needed to overcome her shyness. Normally that bothered Ruthie, but today she didn't mind.

Ruthie had just straightened a couple of the shelves where Papa had pushed some merchandise aside to count stock when she heard the door open. She glanced up in time to see a short, blond-haired woman wearing a dark gray skirt, lighter gray long-sleeved blouse, and a crocheted hair cover walk in.

"Hi," Ruthie said. She suspected the woman might be Rosemary, but she didn't want to assume anything. "May I help you?"

"Is Mr. Kauffman here? My name is Rosemary, and I think he's expecting me."

Until this moment, Ruthie didn't think she'd ever

met anyone shyer than she was, but Rosemary looked frightened. Her heart went out to the woman.

"I'm Ruthie Kauffman, his daughter. Papa said if you arrived before he came back from the bank, I should show you around the store."

Rosemary's lips quivered as she smiled. "Okay."

For the first time in her life, Ruthie had the upper hand, making her feel confident and outgoing. "Have you ever worked in a store before?" Ruthie asked.

Rosemary shook her head. "No. The only work I ever did was help people with their children and some light housekeeping."

"You'll need to talk to customers if you work here," Ruthie said. "Can you do that?"

The brief hesitation let Ruthie know Rosemary wasn't sure what to say. "I...um...if you tell me what to say, I think I can."

Ruthie never thought she'd see the day when someone else asked her how to talk to people and help customers in the store. She'd always been self-conscious about doing it before, but Rosemary was counting on her, and Papa wasn't here. If a customer walked in, she'd have to act confident.

She continued showing Rosemary around. As they walked by the front window, Ruthie leaned over and glanced down the street. Papa sure was taking his time. She didn't see any signs of him.

A middle-aged couple walked in and asked if they carried anything they could bring back home to their granddaughter. As Rosemary watched, Ruthie asked how old the child was and if she liked animals. Once she had the answers, she showed the couple some children's T-shirts, an alligator pencil, and a juice cup shaped like an orange. The couple bought all the items and walked out of the store happy that they didn't have to go anywhere else.

"You make it look so easy," Rosemary said. "I'm not sure I can be that good with people."

"Sure you can. Remember that the customers aren't grading you. They're thinking about what souvenir to buy and take home to show that they've been to Florida." Papa had told Ruthie this so many times she had it memorized. "Tell you what. When Papa comes back, I can show you the books. After we go over that, we can come out to the sales floor. You can observe today, and next time you come to work, I'll let you handle the easy customers."

Rosemary blinked, smiled, and nodded. "Thank—"

Papa walked in and caught their attention. "You must be Rosemary." He smiled, but Ruthie could tell something was bothering him.

Chapter Seven

Ruthie told Papa how she'd shown Rosemary around. "And now that you're back, I'd like to show her the books."

A frown replaced his smile for an instant, but he quickly recovered. "That's a good idea. I'll tend to things out here."

Rosemary cast a curious glance toward Ruthie, but she didn't say anything as they walked back to the store office. Once seated, Ruthie behind the desk and Rosemary in a side chair, Ruthie leaned over and saw Papa rubbing the back of his neck. She could tell he was worried about something, but based on how he was acting, she couldn't very well ask about it in front of Rosemary—especially not on her first day.

"Did your uncle tell you how many hours you'd be working?" Ruthie asked. "I knew you were coming, but Papa and I didn't discuss your hours."

"He wasn't sure, but your father said I'd start out

part-time and work up to full-time if I like the job…
and if you and your father like me."

"Oh, I'm sure we'll like you just fine," Ruthie assured her. "Wait right here. I'm going to ask Papa
how long he wants you here today."

Ruthie found Papa in one of the aisles. He was
bent over, counting items on a shelf where he'd left
off earlier.

She touched his shoulder. "Papa, I have a couple
of questions."

He quickly stood and grazed his head on the edge
of the shelf. "Be careful when you come up from
behind. You startled me." His angry tone alarmed
Ruthie, and she took a step back. Even if he'd
slammed his head on the shelf, he didn't typically
get mad about something like that.

"I'm so sorry, Papa." She reached toward him and
gently rubbed his back.

"Neh, Ruthie, I'm the one who should be sorry.
There was no reason for me to talk to you like that.
What do you need?"

"I've shown Rosemary the sales floor, and now
we're going over the books. Is there anything else
you wanted me to do with her?"

He shook his head. "I think that should be it for
today."

"How many hours do you want her to work?"

Papa rubbed his chin as he thought about it.
Ruthie glanced around the shelf and saw Rosemary
still sitting in the same position, still as a statue.

"All depends. I would like her to eventually be

full-time, but not now. How about twenty hours a week until she's comfortable working here?"

"I'll tell her."

"Have her come in five mornings a week and make sure Saturdays are included."

"I'll give her a schedule," Ruthie agreed. She started to walk back to the office but paused a few steps away. "Papa, what is wrong?"

"I can tell you later."

"At least give me a hint, okay?"

His jaw tightened before he finally nodded. "I ran into Howard Krahn at the bank. He said he and some of the others are going to see to it that the Polk family leaves the church."

"But why would they do that?"

"He questions Jonathan Polk's motives. Claims Jonathan is using the church."

"What is there to use? It's not like we're giving them anything besides friendship."

Papa gave her a half smile. "I know. But you know that the Krahns have quite a bit of clout, and Howard can be very convincing."

"Ya, I do know that, but I think the people in the church are kind and loving enough to accept those who are sincere in wanting to be part of the fold."

"Howard is coming here this afternoon to talk to me some more. I think it would be best if Rosemary left before that."

"What time?" Ruthie asked.

"He said late, so tell her she can leave at two."

"Do you still want me to take her to lunch at Penner's?"

"Ya," he said, "tell you what. Take her to lunch at one after the crowd has a chance to die down. I will pay her for the time since you will probably discuss the store and answer any questions she has."

Ruthie brought the information back to Rosemary, who still hadn't moved. Some of the fear appeared to have subsided, but she was still obviously nervous.

The bookkeeping system wasn't complicated, so it didn't take long for Ruthie to show her how to balance the numbers. "I can show you a couple of times; then we'll work together before I turn you loose on it."

Rosemary nodded. "I'm wondering something, Ruthie."

"What's that?"

"Since you have been doing this for so long, and you obviously know what you're doing, why does your father want me to learn this?"

Ruthie wondered the same thing, but she wasn't about to let on. "I think he wants backup, just in case something happens and I can't do this anymore."

"Oh." Rosemary still didn't look convinced.

"It's never a bad idea to have more than one person who knows how to do a job. We also need more salespeople to work in the store during busy seasons."

"I just hope I am able to help." She glanced down shyly. "I'm not exactly the most outgoing person."

Ruthie smiled. "After you learn the job, you will

do just fine. Would you like to see the ordering process now? Papa generally handles it, but there are times when he's swamped and I have to jump in and help."

Ruthie went over how to do inventory and ordering. Rosemary didn't say much, so Ruthie assumed she understood. By the time one o'clock came, Ruthie had shown Rosemary most of the operation of the store.

"Ready for lunch?"

Rosemary gave her a shy smile. "Ya, I am very hungry."

Papa handed Ruthie some cash to treat Rosemary to lunch. "You don't need to come back to the shop," he told Ruthie. "I don't expect a crowd."

"Mr. Krahn's coming," she reminded him. "You might need me to tend the shop while you talk to him."

"I don't have anything to say to him. If I am alone in the shop, I will have work to do." He fixed her with a firm gaze. "The more I think about it, the more I know it is wrong for him to do this."

Ruthie could tell he knew what he needed to do. "Okay, I'll go home and help Mother."

Rosemary stood by the door watching. Ruthie joined her, and they walked to Penner's in silence.

Charles kept watch for David while Pop packed their lunches. Mom had already left for her job, so the house was quiet. In the past, either Pop or Charles turned on the TV first thing just to have noise in the house. Over time since working for Abe, they'd gradually gotten out of the habit.

David showed up a couple of minutes early as usual. He said he'd rather wait than keep someone else waiting.

All the way to the farm, Pop and David discussed the various crops while Charles partly listened but mostly thought about something he'd been considering for a while. School had become less important to him, and he loved working on the farm. He wondered what Mom and Pop would say if he told them he wanted to quit his studies and work for Abe full-time. Abe could obviously use the help.

David occasionally glanced at Charles in the rearview mirror. "You okay back there? You're awfully quiet."

"I'm fine. Just doing some thinking."

David laughed. "Sometimes my wife tells me I think too much."

Pop glanced over his shoulder from the front passenger seat. "Are you worried about something, Charles? You've been awful quiet lately—even at home."

Charles lifted a shoulder in a half shrug. He didn't think this was the time or place to discuss his future.

"Not worried exactly," Charles said slowly. "We can talk about it later."

David cast another quick glance in the mirror before changing the subject. "Looks like we might get some rain this afternoon. Want me to pick you up early?"

"I'll call you if we do," Pop said. "Abe might need us for some chores in the house or barn."

Charles kept his eyes peeled on the farmland as they approached Abe's place. The change in scenery—from touristy beach town to the farms and land waiting to be farmed—wrapped him in a sense of peace. He felt as though he'd been living in two completely different worlds since they'd been attending the Mennonite church. Eventually he'd have to make a decision between the two, and at the moment, the simple life won hands down. It was difficult to keep his eyes focused on the Lord when his schoolwork led him in a more worldly direction. He sometimes wondered how Abe had managed to go all the way through college without losing some of who he was.

As soon as they pulled up in front of the farmhouse, Abe walked outside and stepped down off the porch. He leaned over and chatted with David while Charles and his pop got out of the car. David pulled away, and the men went into the house to put their lunches on the kitchen counter.

"I told David to come early today. We will get as much work done this morning as possible; then you can go on home. I'm taking Mary and the baby into town, so I thought it would be a good idea to make one trip instead of two."

Pop nodded. "I have plenty to keep me busy at home with some things Lori wants done around the house."

"Have you decided what to do about your house

yet?" Abe asked as they started their trek toward the barn.

"We have to get caught up before we make any decisions," Pop replied.

"Ya, that is a good idea for business purposes. If potential buyers know you are behind, they might try to take advantage of you." He unbolted the barn door and opened it wide. "We have been praying that you make a wise decision."

"So have we," Pop said as he cast a brief glimpse in Charles's direction. "Lori and I pray about it every night. At first I was concerned she wouldn't be okay with moving out of her dream house, but now she says her dream has turned into a nightmare."

"That happens," Abe said. "Particularly when we try to tell the Lord what we want without listening to what He wants for us."

All morning Charles thought about Abe's words. In the past, Mom and Pop spent all their time planning for a future filled with everything money could buy. They didn't even bother waiting until they had the money either. Instead they charged everything to their credit cards, assuming the money would always be there. Although he hadn't heard his parents fighting, he sensed their tension as their concern about making ends meet increased.

What he now found amazing was the way the heated discussions had subsided. They still disagreed, but instead of letting the arguments escalate, they turned to prayer. The problems didn't disappear, but with God's direction, they'd begun to take action in lowering their debt. And instead of turning Charles down as they once had when he offered his financial assistance, they accepted. Pop had once told him he had too much pride to allow his son to pay the bills. Charles appreciated being able to help out. It made him feel more like the man he knew he was.

They broke for lunch and headed down toward one of the lakes on the edge of Abe's property. Some of the other farmhands chose to stay in the backyard, but Charles wanted to talk to Pop in private.

"What's on your mind, son?" Pop asked as he leaned against a tree, sandwich in hand.

Charles chewed his bottom lip then decided to just let his thoughts out. "I'm thinking about dropping out of school."

Pop didn't even flinch. "I thought you might wind up doing this."

"Are you okay with it? We always talked about how important education was."

"Education is important," Pop said. "But that doesn't mean you have to stay in a college program that doesn't lead you to anything you want to do. You can't keep taking classes without a goal in mind." He turned and faced Charles. "So have you decided exactly what you want to do…besides being a clown?" A smile played on his lips.

Charles laughed. "That was a rather silly dream, wasn't it?"

"Not really. There are plenty of clowns who do quite well."

That was one of the things Charles always appreciated about Pop. Although in the past he'd stressed the importance of education, if Charles wanted to do something, he was able to do it without parental resistance.

"I love working on Abe's farm," Charles said. He finished the last of his sandwich and opened his bag of chips. "It gives me such a good feeling at the end of a long day."

"Yeah, I know exactly how you feel. I like it, too." Pop rolled up his empty chip bag and extracted a cookie from his lunch box. "Why don't you finish the semester and take some time off?"

Charles didn't want to finish the semester, but he understood what Pop was saying. "Okay."

"After we sell the house—that is, if we can find someone to buy it—maybe we can think about buying some land."

Charles thought about the bills they still owed. "Maybe we can live in town and continue working here until all the bills are paid off."

Pop chuckled. "Good thinking. I like the idea of not having all those bills hanging over my head."

"What's your thinking about the church?" Charles asked. He'd been wondering about this, and now seemed a good time to bring it up.

"You do realize there are some people there who don't trust us, right?" Pop said. "I don't want to impose on anyone who doesn't want me."

"The Lord wants you," Charles said, "and that's all that really matters."

Pop looked out over the horizon before turning

back to Charles and patting his shoulder. "I don't know how this happened, but my son is getting smarter than his old man."

"That'll never happen." Charles closed his lunch box, stood, and dusted off the back of his jeans. "Let's get back so we can finish up before David comes to pick us up."

As they walked back to the Glicks' backyard, Charles inhaled the fragrance of plants and fresh dirt. He couldn't remember anything smelling this good.

An hour and a half later, they were in David's van heading back to town. Mary spoke quietly with Abe in the middle seat, their baby in a car seat in the middle section, while Charles and Pop stared out the side windows.

Ruthie noticed how quiet Papa was during supper. Mother occasionally glanced back and forth between Papa and Ruthie, but she didn't say anything. Finally when she got up to serve dessert, Papa motioned for her to sit back down.

"I would like to discuss some things with the two of you," he said.

"Can't it wait?" Mother asked.

"Neh. I would like to do it now."

Mother folded her hands in her lap and nodded. Ruthie could tell Mother already knew what was going on. She turned to Papa. "What is so important that we have to talk about it now?"

"I spoke with Howard Krahn this afternoon. He seems to think the reason we are not opposed to the

Polks joining the church has something to do with Charles courting you."

"We're not exactly courting." Ruthie glanced down at the table as her cheeks flamed.

Papa propped his elbows on the table and steepled his fingers. "That is not the way people in the church see things."

"Why would that be a problem?" Mother asked. "I would think that would make people appreciate the Polks even more."

"Not the way they look at it," Papa said. "Howard seems to think we stand a good chance of losing Ruthie to the world if she continues seeing Charles." He turned and faced Ruthie with a long gaze before shaking his head and turning back to Mother. "Our daughter has a good head on her shoulders. I don't see her leaving the church for any man. Besides, if the Polks are sincere—and I think they are—it is a decision that requires many hours of hard work and effort."

"Ya," Mother agreed. "I don't think someone who wasn't sincere would go to that much trouble."

Ruthie listened to her parents discussing the Polks and decided this was probably not a good time to continue pursuing a relationship with Charles—at least not until they were sure. If his family wound up not joining the church, she'd be an emotional mess. As it was, she liked him enough to know she'd miss him if she didn't see him again. On the other hand, if his family eventually became accepted members, she was still young and she had plenty of time to court Charles—that is, if he wanted to.

"Well?" Papa asked, staring at her. "What do you think about it?"

She blinked. "Sorry, Papa. I wasn't listening."

He leaned back in his chair, folded his arms, and feigned anger. "Not listening? What kind of daughter doesn't listen?" Before she could respond, he burst out laughing. "Thinking about the young man again? I understand." He reached for Mother's hand. "We were young once."

Ruthie needed to set her parents straight. "I like Charles, but I've decided I need to back off…at least for now. There is no point in continuing to see him if I'm not sure he'll even stay."

Papa gave her an odd glance. "Have you prayed about this?"

She couldn't lie, so she shook her head. "No, Papa, but I don't think the Lord wants me taking chances like this."

"Ruthie, the Lord wants you to turn to Him for everything, including matters of the heart, which doesn't mean you can't take chances. If you care about Charles as much as I think you do, you should turn to God and ask for guidance. Don't try to make any decisions without Him."

Papa was right, but Ruthie didn't know where to start with a prayer about her relationship—particularly since she wasn't certain how Charles felt about her. She didn't have enough experience with men to even begin figuring them out.

"That is what your Mother and I will pray for, Ruthie. And I want you to remember to do the same."

After dinner all three of them cleared the dishes. Mother filled the sink with water, and Papa went out to the backyard to check on his tomatoes that had been attacked by aphids.

"Ruthie, do you mind bringing me the salt-shaker?" Mother asked. "The humidity has the holes blocked, and I need to clear them out."

They worked in silence as they finished cleaning the kitchen. Once they were finished, Ruthie went out the front door and watched the sun set.

A few minutes after the sun went down, Papa joined her on the porch. "Rosemary seems like a nice girl. Do you think she can handle the store?"

"She caught on to the paperwork fairly quickly, but she seems timid around the customers," Ruthie replied.

Pop looked down at Ruthie. "You were that girl once, remember?"

She smiled. "I still am."

"And you do just fine with the customers, so I suspect she will, too."

He had an excellent point, and she nodded. "True."

"My concern is how motivated she is to make the effort."

"I'll try to find out," Ruthie offered. "She said she likes it here."

"That's a good start. Why don't you get your office work done early and spend more time with her on the sales floor tomorrow?"

* * *

The next morning Charles decided to leave the house early and stop by the Kauffmans' souvenir shop before going to the campus. He was surprised to see another woman standing behind the counter. As he approached, he thought he saw fear in her eyes. His heart sank as he assumed she must be one of the people from the church he hadn't met yet.

"M-may I help you?" she asked as he got closer.

"Is Ruthie around?"

"Um…she stepped out for just a few minutes. Would you like me to give her a message?"

"Do you think she'll be back in the next five minutes or so?" She nodded. "I think so."

"Good, then I'll wait."

As Charles walked around and perused the aisles, he couldn't help but smile at some of the merchandise. The store offered everything from scented orange-shaped erasers to chocolate alligators. He imagined tourists buying some of those items and wondering what to do with them once they got home.

"Charles?"

The sound of Ruthie's voice from behind caught his attention. He turned and found himself face-to-face with Ruthie, and his breath caught in his throat. The sweet expression on her face had captured his heart, and he suspected he'd never be able to erase the image of her soulful eyes looking at him at this moment.

"Hi, Ruthie. I just wanted to stop by and see you for a few minutes before I go to class."

"Did you need something?" she asked as she took a step back.

Charles looked around, trying to think of something to say. His gaze settled on the other woman in the store. "Who is she?"

"Oh, that's Rosemary. Papa hired her to help out, and I'm training her."

"I don't think I've met her," Charles said. "Does she go to our—I mean, your church?"

Ruthie studied him for a second before replying. "She just moved here, but I think she will go to our church."

Charles was at a loss for words. In the past, he would have resorted to putting on a clown act, but he didn't want to do that with Ruthie. She'd see right through him.

He lifted his arm and glanced at his watch. "Well, I better get going. I have to catch the next bus to make it to class on time."

Chapter Eight

After Charles left, Ruthie turned and walked toward Rosemary. "Did you have any problems while I was gone?"

"No," Rosemary said. "That man you were just talking to was the only person who came in."

Ruthie cleared her throat. "Tuesdays are generally slow. Papa should be here shortly. Once he arrives, we can place the order. I'll let you do it."

"But—"

"You'll do just fine. I'll be right there with you to make sure you don't make any mistakes."

Having someone to teach gave Ruthie confidence she didn't know she possessed, even though she sensed something else going on with Rosemary. Papa had trusted her, and now she was happy to rise to the occasion. But she made a mental note to be cautious.

After Papa came into the store, Ruthie and Rosemary spent the rest of the time going through the new catalogs and ordering merchandise. "Until you learn your way around here, it's probably best to concentrate on reorders of what we know sells," she explained. "Papa likes to add new merchandise, but he's very careful about which vendors he chooses. Some of them aren't as reputable as others, and we won't carry merchandise that doesn't fit what we believe."

Ruthie was happy to see that Rosemary paid close attention and asked questions. Occasionally she caught Rosemary giving her an odd look, but she didn't mention it. Instead she found something else to explain.

Dan Hostetler from one of the neighboring shops stopped by right before noon. "I saw the Polk boy come in here earlier," he told Papa.

Ruthie quickly stilled as she waited for Papa's reaction. It was Rosemary, however, who broke into a coughing fit. "I'll get you some water," Ruthie offered.

"No," Rosemary said. "I'll be fine."

Papa frowned at Rosemary before responding to Mr. Hostetler. "I didn't know the Polk boy was here, but that is fine by me. Did you have anything else to say about it?"

"No," Mr. Hostetler said, shaking his head while staring at Ruthie through narrowed eyes. "I just thought you needed to know since you weren't in the store at the time."

"He can come in here anytime the store is open," Papa said. "Is there anything else I can do for you?"

Mr. Hostetler mumbled a few words about evil trying to infiltrate the church before leaving. Ruthie noticed Papa's jaw tightening.

Ruthie wished Rosemary wouldn't stare at her. She felt as though Rosemary was judging her.

Papa went back to the office, leaving the women on the sales floor. Ruthie decided to explain stock rotation and other merchandising concepts since they were still so slow.

After a half hour, Ruthie had taught her everything she knew about merchandising. Rosemary still looked puzzled.

"Is there anything you still don't understand?" Ruthie asked.

"One thing," Rosemary said. "Is it always this slow around here?"

"No, it's just that way early in the week and during the times between our tourist seasons."

"When are the tourist seasons?" Rosemary asked.

"Holidays are generally busy. We see a lot of older people during the winter, and then families come when their children get out of school in the summertime."

Rosemary nodded. "I guess you probably don't have many customers who are from Sarasota."

"Actually we have quite a few. Some people like to buy Florida souvenirs for family and friends up north."

Ruthie hadn't realized how much she knew about her family's business until Rosemary asked all those questions. The extra confidence boost made her feel good.

"I have one more question," Rosemary said softly.

Fully expecting it to be about business, Ruthie looked at Rosemary. "What's that?"

"Why are you courting that Polk man? My uncle

says he's not Mennonite, and if he has anything to do with it, he and his family won't be allowed to join the church."

For a shy girl, Rosemary sure did know how to produce a shock. Ruthie felt her blood rush as she tried to think of an answer. She opened her mouth but nothing came out. Fortunately Papa walked up and took over.

"All done here?" he asked. Instead of waiting for an answer, he gave a clipped nod toward the door. "You can go on home now, Rosemary. We'll see you in the morning."

He folded his arms and waited for Rosemary to get her bag. As soon as she left, he turned to Ruthie. "How long has she been talking about the Polks?"

"Not long," Ruthie replied. "She just asked—"

"I heard what she asked," Papa said. "She has no business coming into our store and talking to you like that."

"She surprised me."

"Next time she says anything about her uncle's opinion of the Polk family, tell me right away so I can deal with it. I would have said something this time, but I wanted to find out what you'd already told her first."

Ruthie swallowed hard and nodded. "Okay, Papa."

Fortunately the summer semester was a short one. Charles didn't think he could last much longer in the classes that had ceased to hold his interest a long time ago. He studied hard during the next couple of weeks to get good grades, in case he ever decided to go back to school.

When he first mentioned his desires to Abe, he was surprised at Abe's reaction. "Don't do anything you'll regret. I agree with your father. Finish the semester and make sure you do it on good terms. You may decide to finish your education, and getting low grades will make it more difficult to come back."

"Would you consider hiring me full-time?" Charles asked. "I mean, I like the work, and we could use the mon—"

"Ya, I need more labor. I will switch you to full-time as soon as you finish this semester." The pleased look on Abe's face overshadowed his stern voice.

Charles wanted to jump for joy, but he tamped down his excitement as much as he could. "Thanks, Abe."

The rest of the afternoon Charles had more energy than ever. Pop walked up to him and laughed. "I want some of whatever you ate for lunch. You're working circles around the rest of us."

"I don't want Abe to regret offering me full-time work after this semester," Charles said without bothering to hide his smile.

"Good job, son. I never dreamed you and I would be working together, let alone doing farm labor."

"The Lord is amazing, isn't He?"

Pop took a long look at Charles before placing his hand on his shoulder. "Yes, He is amazing, but we still have quite a few hurdles."

"That's only because we're dealing with imperfect people," Charles reminded him. "Too bad others aren't as understanding as Abe."

"Most of them are open to our joining the church," Pop said.

"Do you think that the minority can keep us out?"

Pop shook his head. "I don't know, but one thing I'm certain of is that the Lord knows what's in our hearts. If we aren't allowed into this church, we are to ask for guidance and direction." He glanced up and pointed. "Here comes Abe."

"I've been thinking about asking Abe for advice on how to handle the people who are trying to keep us out."

"No, let's not do that yet, Charles. There's no point in creating controversy among his friends."

"Shouldn't we at least tell him what's going on?"

"He probably already knows." Pop lifted a hand and waved to Abe. "Looks like we're right on schedule," he called out.

"Ya. You are both doing a fine job. I have a good crew."

Charles felt pride swell in his chest before remembering the One to thank. He silently sent up a prayer, and when he opened his eyes, he noticed Abe watching him.

"Finished with your prayer?" Abe said.

Charles nodded, both Abe and Pop looking at him. "I sure wish I could come tomorrow, but I still have classes."

"How much longer before this semester is over?" Abe asked.

"Three more weeks."

"Good. You'll be done in time to work full-time on the fall harvest and get ready for the citrus. Jeremiah said that if you finish early he can use you over at his place."

Charles and Pop both liked working for Jeremiah, who was just as fair as Abe. Jeremiah's wife, Shelley, was working on getting their new house in order before the baby arrived. Charles occasionally wondered how difficult it had been for Jeremiah to transition back to the simple Mennonite life after being out in the world for several years.

"Looks like David's here." Abe shielded his eyes against the late-afternoon sun and pointed toward the shell-covered driveway. "I'll see you tomorrow, Jonathan." He turned and walked back toward the house.

The instant the Polk driveway was in sight, Charles saw Pop frown. "The garage door is open." They got closer and the frown turned to a look of worry. "Looks like your mother is home early today. That's odd."

"I'm sure everything is okay, Pop. She probably finished work and got sent home. Mom said they've been cutting hours."

David pulled into the driveway and stopped. "I'll be here first thing in the morning, Jonathan. Call if you need me before then."

Charles and Pop got out and made it halfway up the walk when the door flew open and Mom came running out, tears streaming down her cheeks. Pop pulled her to his chest and wrapped his arms around her, leaving Charles standing there looking on.

"What happened, Lori?" Pop asked.

"They had to let a bunch of people go." She dabbed at her tear-stained cheeks with a wadded tissue. "What are we gonna do, Jonathan? You and Charles aren't making nearly enough to support us. We have to get this house ready to sell."

Pop's worry lines deepened, but he didn't let it come through in his voice. "We'll figure out something. Right now let's go inside and pray about it."

In the past, prayer would have been an afterthought. Pop gently helped Mom to the sofa, and he sat down next to her. Charles took the chair adjacent to them. Between sniffles, Mom told Charles and Pop how her boss had taken her and several of her coworkers to lunch. She knew something wasn't right because they'd discontinued company-funded lunches during cutbacks.

"Did he tell you before or after you ate?" Pop asked.

Mom gave him a curious look. "Afterward. Why?"

Pop shrugged. "At least he let you enjoy the food."

Her chin quivered. "Now what am I supposed to do? It's hard to get a job in these times."

Charles remembered meeting someone new at the Kauffmans' shop. "Maybe you can ask someone at church. Some of the businesses around Pinecraft seem to be doing just fine."

"All I know is office work," she said.

Pop pulled her to her feet. "We can ask around.

I'm sure we'll be just fine. Take a few days and try to calm down a bit before you start looking."

The following Sunday, Ruthie went to church with her parents, determined not to get in the position of being alone with Charles. It was too risky now that she'd been with him and knew how he could make her feel.

Mother was the first to notice Mrs. Polk standing alone, looking forlorn. "She's usually such a happy person. Let's go check on her." Before Ruthie had a chance to say a word, Mother had made a beeline to Charles's mother.

Ruthie started to follow, but Charles stepped from out of nowhere and into her path. "Can we talk for a minute?"

"Um…" Ruthie cut her glance over toward her mother who had Mrs. Polk cornered. They were deep in conversation. "I guess that's okay."

"My family needs your prayers. Mom lost her job last week. Dad and I are both working, but without Mom's paycheck, I'm not sure how we'll pay our bills."

Prayer. That much she could do. "Of course I'll pray for your family."

"I offered to quit school so I could get more hours right away, but Pop and Abe still don't want me to drop out."

"I'm sure they have a good reason." Ruthie couldn't even pretend to understand the stress of having to pay bills. She wasn't even twenty yet, and she'd always lived with her parents who'd always lived a frugal lifestyle.

"We want to sell the house and get out from under all our debt, but it's hard with all the bills we've incurred."

"I can imagine." But she really couldn't. She glanced over toward Mr. Polk, who was deep in conversation with Abe by the church door. "I'll pray for your family," she repeated, "but now I need to get settled in for church."

Charles pursed his lips and stepped to the side. "Yes, of course. Maybe we can talk later?"

"Maybe." She scurried toward a pew near where Mother still stood with Mrs. Polk. A few minutes later the two women joined her.

Mother leaned over and whispered, "Lori lost her job last week."

"Yes, I know," Ruthie said. "Charles just told me."

"I'm going to ask around and see if anyone is hiring. All she knows how to do is paperwork, but she's young enough to learn something new." Mother stared straight ahead for a few seconds before turning back to Ruthie with her eyebrows raised. "I wonder if your papa would want to hire her for the store."

"He just hired Rosemary, remember?"

"Oh, that's right. I'm not so sure he's all that pleased with Rosemary, but I don't think he will ever send her away without a good solid reason."

Ruthie agreed with a nod. "Rosemary doesn't seem to mind working in the back, but she's not happy about helping customers."

Mother grimaced. "That's one of the things she'll need to change if she wants to continue working in retail."

Ruthie wondered if Papa had told Mother what he'd overheard Rosemary say. He'd always been a man of his word, no matter what—even when angry—so Mother was right about him keeping Rosemary employed.

Charles thought the semester would never end, but the day of his final exams finally arrived. Abe gave him an extra day off to study, so he had no excuse not to do well. After he finished the last exam, he felt light on his feet as he walked across campus toward the bus stop.

He couldn't wait to start working full-time for Abe, and now that he was free from school—at least for now—he'd be able to do that the following week. Mom was even more stressed over losing her job. She'd taken a few days off at Pop's insistence, but now she went out every morning and applied at all the companies where she thought she was qualified to work. Charles noticed that she started out with hope, but as time went on without a nibble, her spirit had started to fade.

As he waited at the bus stop, he said a silent prayer for Mom—not only that she'd find work, but that her mood would be lifted. Mom had always been one of the most positive people he'd ever known, so this was a side of her he'd never seen. Even when she and

Pop had started worrying about paying bills, they at least had hope for a breakthrough. Seeing her beaten down broke his heart.

No one was home when Charles arrived, so he went around the house and did some straightening up. He still had some pent-up energy left, so he vacuumed, ran the dishwasher, and when the dishes were clean, unloaded it. Then he thought it might be nice to start supper. He wasn't a great cook, but he could put together a basic meal. Their stock in the pantry had slowly diminished over time, making meal planning difficult.

Charles had a few dollars in his pocket, but they lived too far from a grocery store to walk. He thought about how easy life would be if they were in a community such as Pinecraft, where he could walk almost anywhere he wanted to go.

He took one more look in the pantry and decided to make a chicken casserole with the condensed cream soup, the small amount of rice in the container, and some chicken thighs he saw in the freezer. Pop had brought home some green beans and tomatoes from Abe's farm, so he could prepare a full meal.

Pop got home first. He walked in the door, sniffed the air, and shot Charles a puzzled look. "I didn't see the car. Is your mom home?"

"No, I started supper."

"Good for you." Pop washed his hands at the kitchen sink. "I hope this is a good sign for your mother. She's determined to find something even though I told her to try not to stress over it so much."

"I know but she's always worked."

Pop tightened his lips and nodded. "That's another thing I wish we'd done differently. When we first got married, she said she wanted to be a full-time mother to our children as long as they remained at home, but there were so many things we wanted, it became impossible after a while."

"Don't beat yourself up over it, Pop. You both did what you thought was right, and I turned out just fine."

Pop stepped closer to Charles and placed his hand on his shoulder. "You sure did, son. I'm very proud of you."

Mom arrived home a few minutes before it was time to remove the casserole from the oven. For the first time in weeks, she beamed.

"Good news! I finally found a job." She cleared her throat before adding, "It's not exactly what I'm qualified to do, but it's something I should be able to learn fairly quickly."

"Are you gonna keep us in suspense all night?" Pop asked. She grinned as she glanced back and forth between Charles and Pop. "Joseph Penner hired me to work the breakfast shift."

"Breakfast shift? As in waiting tables?" Pop asked. His jaw fell slack.

"Yep. I never thought I'd be this excited about working in a restaurant, but on a whim I decided to ask if he knew of any job openings. Apparently Shelley and Jeremiah are getting ready to move out to their farm, and it will be difficult for her to stay at the restaurant. She agreed to stay long enough to train me."

"Mom, that's wonderful," Charles said as he closed the distance between them for a hug. "Mr. Penner seems like a fair man."

"The salary isn't great, but Jocelyn said the tips are the best she's ever gotten. Apparently they have a mix of regular customers and tourists, so I'll never be bored."

Pop remained standing in the same spot, staring at Mom with a neutral expression. Charles couldn't tell what he was thinking.

"Say something, Jonathan," Mom said. "You're not upset, are you?"

He shook his head. "Not upset, but are you sure you want to do this? Waiting tables is hard work."

"No harder than anything else I've ever done. And it's something I can do and then come home and forget about it."

"That's a good thing," Pop agreed. "Ever since I've worked on the farm, I've slept like a baby."

Mom smiled at him. "That's what I'm counting on. I'm tired of not sleeping at night. And at least now we'll all have an income, so we should be able to keep our heads above water."

"We have to be careful though," Pop reminded her. "Even with all three of us working, our income is still a fraction of what it was."

"Oh," she said as she hung her purse on the hook by the door, "another perk is that I get to take home leftover desserts."

Charles grinned. "And they have the best desserts. Speaking of food, I want you two to sit down. Dinner is almost ready."

As she sat, Mom winked at Charles. "I could get used to this."

Pop said the blessing before Charles put the filled plates on the table. Mom took one bite of her chicken, closed her eyes, and visibly relaxed.

Dinnertime conversation was quite a bit lighter than it had been since Mom lost her job. Charles sent up a silent prayer of thanks.

Ruthie went to church early on Sunday to set up some tables for the potluck. Mom was still preparing the vegetable platter and casserole when she left.

She arrived at the church, expecting to see only a few of the men who generally put the tables on the lawn. When she spotted Charles and his parents talking to the Penners, her breath caught in her throat. She'd managed to avoid Charles by getting lost in the crowd at church, but now, with just a few people there, it would be awkward.

The second Charles spotted her, he left his parents and came toward her. There was no way she could even pretend not to see him.

"I've missed you, Ruthie," he said. "We need to talk."

"Maybe later. I have to cover the tables and set up the condiments for the potluck."

Charles lifted his hands. "I'll help."

Each time they made eye contact or brushed

hands, her heart hammered and her mouth went dry. There was no way she could deny the attraction she'd tried to push aside. After they finished their tasks, Charles brushed his hands together. "All done. See? When you have two people working, you can get everything done in half the time. Now can we talk?"

She couldn't very well say no so she nodded. Charles led her over to a bench beneath the shade tree on the edge of the church lawn.

"I'm working full-time for Abe now," he said.

She looked him in the eye. "You quit school? For good?"

He shrugged. "Maybe. Abe said I might want to go back later, but for now I've decided I prefer working on the farm all day."

"You've really taken to farming, haven't you?"

He nodded. "I love everything about it."

"Even more than being a clown?" she teased.

"Way more than being a clown. It feels more like a calling from the Lord."

Ruthie studied his expression as he explained all the things he enjoyed about working on the farm—from the physical labor to the beauty of the land. There was no doubt in her mind that he was sincere.

"Ruthie," he said softly before pausing. When she met his gaze, he took one of her hands and covered it with his. "I really like you…a lot. Is there any way we can hang out more and see where our relationship can go?"

Chapter Nine

She hadn't expected such a direct question. "I…
uh, I'll have to talk to Mother and Papa." She already knew her parents would be fine with her seeing
Charles, as long as she did so in a cautious manner,
but she'd already decided to back off.

He nodded. "Of course I want to date you with
their blessing. It wouldn't be right to do it any other
way."

Ruthie wondered if Charles was aware of the people who disapproved. But not everyone was against
it. In fact, some of her parents' friends who'd arrived
at church early had seen her talking to Charles and
were grinning. She knew it wouldn't be long before
the matchmaking resumed. And the heated discussions would continue.

"I hear you're having a birthday soon." Charles
met her gaze with a grin. "Would you like to do
something special?"

Ruthie had always had a quiet birthday dinner

at home. "I don't know what Mother and Papa have planned."

"I wouldn't want to interfere with whatever it is, so perhaps you and I can go out on a different day?"

His persistence flattered her, and she couldn't resist her heart's desire. "What would you want to do?" she asked. "I enjoyed the circus, but I don't think I want to do that for my birthday."

Charles looked away then back at her. "To be honest, I'm not sure what all we're allowed to do."

Ruthie's heart warmed at his admission. "We could go on that picnic we talked about or…" She hesitated for a moment. "I've always wanted to go to an art gallery."

"Then let's do that," Charles said. "The Ringling Museum of Art is one of the best I've ever seen."

In spite of her resolve, Ruthie decided right then and there to throw caution to the wind. "I would love to go!"

As soon as the words left Charles's mouth, he regretted asking Ruthie to go to the Ringling Museum of Art. Money was tight, and although he'd never considered the admission price too high, it was money they needed to pay bills. But there was no way he could retract his offer now that he'd made it.

They chatted a few more minutes until it was time to go into the church. Pop nudged him. "So how's Ruthie?"

Charles cleared his throat. "Fine."

Pop leaned away from Charles and narrowed his

eyes. "What's wrong, son? Did you two have an argument?"

Charles didn't want to mention his concern about asking Ruthie to do something he couldn't afford. "No, we had a nice talk." He gestured toward the pastor who had walked up to the front of the church.

As they worshipped and prayed, Charles tried to focus on the service. Every once in a while a sense of dread washed over him. He couldn't back out of his offer to take Ruthie to the art museum, but his family needed every penny he earned at the Glick farm, so he had to figure out something else.

After church Mr. Penner chatted with Mom and Pop and said he was happy to have her working in his restaurant. The chasm between the groups who were for and against the Polk family joining the church had become wider and more obvious. Those who didn't like the idea of outsiders becoming one of them walked a wide berth around all three of them, while those who welcomed them didn't hesitate to surround them and offer prayers. Charles could see that these people weren't as different from outsiders as he used to think. Charles sought out Ruthie after the service was over and asked if she would sit with him. Her brief hesitation made his stomach ache. He wanted her to feel something for him, and he was still confused by her reactions. Sometimes when he caught her looking at him, he thought she might feel an attraction, but other times—like now—he wondered if she was simply being kind.

After the pastor said the blessing, everyone

crowded around the buffet tables. Ruthie helped serve some of the children so Charles waited until she was ready to prepare her own plate. Together they walked to the picnic table farthest from the church.

"Any idea who cooked the ham?" he asked.

"Probably Mary. She generally brings the meat, and her grandparents bring desserts."

"It's seasoned just right." Charles tasted a few other things on his plate. "What did you bring?"

"Mother made the vegetable casserole." She glanced down at his plate before looking at him with a grin. "Looks like you're not big on vegetables."

He wrinkled his nose. "You caught me. Mom used to have to puree my vegetables and put them in sauces, but I have gotten better." He lifted a green bean from his plate. "See? I eat green stuff now."

She laughed aloud. "At least it's a start. Here, try some of my mother's casserole. It's really good." She scooped some of the food off her plate and put it on the edge of his. "Go on, try it."

He studied the blob of food and turned it over with his fork. "Are you sure it's good?"

"It just happens to be my favorite food."

"Okay, then in that case I'll try it." Charles slowly scooped some of the food and lifted it to his lips. "Down the hatch." He put it into his mouth, chewed it, and grinned. "Yeah, for vegetables it's not half bad. And coming from a veggie-phobic, that's a compliment."

A shadow moved over the table so Charles spun

around and saw that Jeremiah and Abe had joined them. "Don't look now," Jeremiah said, "but you two have half the congregation staring at you."

Naturally Charles looked up and saw that Jeremiah was right. "Um…yeah."

Abe sat down beside Charles. "Everyone is interested in what is going on between you two. Enjoying the food?"

Charles cast a quick glance toward Ruthie whose cheeks were flaming red. He felt bad that she was so embarrassed, but at this point there was nothing he could do to change it.

"Yes, the food is delicious. I even tried some vegetables and liked them."

Jeremiah gestured toward someone behind Charles. "Over here, Shelley." He looked down at Charles. "Want me to bring you some dessert?"

Ruthie hopped up. "I can get it. What would you like—pie, cake, or cookies?"

"It all sounds good," Charles said. "Bring me whatever you're having."

Jeremiah's wife, Shelley, and Abe's wife, Mary, joined them and sat across the table from Charles. They instantly started chatting about the baby in Mary's arms and the one Shelley was pregnant with. He was relieved he didn't have to think of anything to say. Jeremiah talked quite a bit, too, but Abe was his usual silent self. He rarely had much to say, but when he spoke, most people listened. For as young as Abe was, Charles could see he garnered a tremendous amount of respect.

For the first time in his life, Charles felt as though he was part of something big. He was surrounded by people who sincerely respected and cared about each other. But when he leaned over and glanced beyond the circle around him, he also saw the doubters—who sat there with pursed lips watching, waiting for the "intruders" to make some sort of mis-step.

Ruthie brought him a plate heaping with a variety of desserts—German chocolate cake, red velvet cake, two kinds of pies, and an oatmeal raisin cookie. He raised his eyebrows and his eyes widened.

Jeremiah laughed. "Better get used to it. These women like to make sure their men are well fed."

Ruthie's face once again turned bright red. Instead of making a big deal over the massive amount of dessert, Charles stabbed a piece of cake and tried it. "This is the best cake I ever had."

"Try the red velvet," Jeremiah said. "You'll like that even better."

Charles had no doubt he'd wind up putting on some weight, which he could stand to do. Most of his life he'd been too skinny anyway, in spite of all the food he put away.

He lost track of time with Ruthie, Abe, Mary, Jeremiah, and Shelley, but eventually the crowd started to disperse. Some of the younger men began breaking down the tables so Charles and his new pals joined in. Ruthie, Mary, and Shelley scurried back and forth carrying bowls and casserole dishes to the kitchen, trying to stay a few steps ahead of the men.

Finally it was time to leave. Ruthie's parents had already gone home so she was there alone.

"Would you like a ride home?" he asked. "I'm sure Mom and Pop won't mind."

She nervously glanced around then shook her head. "Neh, I can walk."

"Are you sure?" he asked.

"Ya. I like to walk."

He watched her walk toward home before joining his parents, who stood near the car patiently waiting. Pop placed his hand on Charles's shoulder, but neither Mom nor Pop said a word about Ruthie all the way home.

Once they were in the house, Charles went straight to his room to try to figure out how he could afford to take Ruthie to the Ringling Museum of Art without sacrificing any of the money his family needed. His gaze settled on his sizable collection of video games. He instantly knew what he needed to do.

It had been a while since he'd been on an Internet auction site, but it didn't take long to list the first batch of items. Rather than list everything at one time, Charles decided to start with a couple dozen CDs and DVDs to see how they'd do. Some of them were rare, so he suspected he'd do well with them. By the time he finished, he already had bids on the first few. He sat back in his chair and stared at the computer screen. A year ago he couldn't imagine himself considering giving up all his electronic gadgets. Now he was eager to move on to a simple life without all the distractions that prevented him from living in the moment and developing a stronger relationship with the Lord.

Later that night as he and his parents sat at the kitchen table eating sandwiches, Pop asked him what he'd been doing all afternoon. "Once we got home, you disappeared."

"I went on an auction site and listed some of my stuff." Charles noticed his parents exchanging a glance as he took another bite of his sandwich. He decided right then to let them in on what he was doing. There was no reason to keep it to himself. "I asked Ruthie to go to the Ringling Museum of Art for her birthday. I can use the money from the sales for that."

Mom's forehead crinkled. "Are you sure you want to do that? I know how much you enjoy your music and movies."

Charles put his sandwich on the plate and leaned back in his chair. "I used to enjoy them, but this whole Mennonite thing…"

Pop chuckled. "Yeah, this *whole Mennonite thing* has me shifting my priorities, too."

"I just hope I get enough to pay for our admission and take Ruthie out for dinner afterward."

Again, Mom and Pop looked at each other before Mom reached for his hand. "We appreciate everything you do, Charles. I don't think we tell you often enough."

Warmth flooded Charles as he smiled back at her. "You are the best parents a guy could have."

"We're not perfect parents though," Mom reminded him. "Perfect parents would be boring." Charles shoved the last bite of sandwich into his mouth and pushed his plate back. "After you're done, why don't you two go for a walk or something? I'll do the dishes."

Pop jumped up from the table and pulled Mom to her feet. "Let's go, Lori, before he changes his mind."

Once Charles was alone in the house, he did the dishes, wiped the countertops, and swept the kitchen floor. In the past, he dreaded the times when Mom asked him to do anything around the house, but now he actually enjoyed it. Once the kitchen was clean, he went to the doorway, turned around to see the fruits of his labor, and smiled. He couldn't remember feeling better about his life.

Ruthie met Rosemary on the sidewalk in front of the shop the next morning so they walked in together. Papa was already inside behind the counter, jotting something onto a notepad.

He glanced up. "Ruthie, I need to talk to you for a few minutes. Rosemary, why don't you mind the floor while my daughter and I meet in the office?"

A panicked look crossed her face. "I...um...okay."

"If you need one of us, just knock on the door," Ruthie said.

Rosemary nodded. She turned her back so Ruthie couldn't see her face anymore, but she knew Rosemary was miserable about being left alone on the sales floor.

Once Papa came into the office and closed the

door behind himself, he turned to Ruthie. "I've been thinking it might be a good idea for you to work for someone else for a while."

"But why?"

Papa shrugged. "This is all you've ever been around. I think another job will give you more perspective."

"What kind of job?"

"Rolf Fresh will be opening a frozen yogurt shop soon, and he's looking for part-time help."

Working in that environment sounded like a nightmare to Ruthie. Not only was she self-conscious out of her element, but she also tended to be klutzy when she was nervous. An image of accidentally dropping a cup or cone of frozen yogurt down a customer's shirt made her shiver with horror.

"I've never done anything like that before," she argued. "That's exactly why I want you to do it." Papa pointed to the chair and waited for her to take a seat before he sat down. "I'm not saying you have to do it forever. I just want you to have more experience than you can get in this store and the housework you do at home. I told Rolf that you'll be there tomorrow for an interview."

"Tomorrow?" Ruthie's voice squeaked.

"Ya." Papa folded his arms. "You'll start next week—that is, if he thinks you can do the work."

All Ruthie could do was nod. After Papa dismissed her, she walked back out to the sales floor where Rosemary remained behind the counter while a couple of customers browsed. Relief replaced Rosemary's panic when she saw Ruthie and her papa coming out of the office.

Since Ruthie was certain her new job was inevitable, she had Rosemary do all the bookwork while she supervised. Papa spent some time telling Rosemary a few simple phrases to use with customers until she became more comfortable.

After lunch, Papa asked Rosemary if she could stay an extra hour. She nodded but Ruthie could tell her heart wasn't in it. Ruthie wondered if Rosemary was as miserable as she was.

By Wednesday, Charles had made enough money off his auctions to take Ruthie to the Ringling Museum of Art and to dinner wherever she wanted to go. And he had money left over that he could give his parents. He was eager to make plans, but now that he worked every day at the farm, he didn't have time. At least he could tell his parents the good news.

"You don't have to give us the money," Pop said. "Keep it for yourself."

"No, Pop. That wouldn't be right. I'm part of this family, too, and I want to share in the responsibility."

Pop started to argue, but Mom shushed him. "Jonathan, I think this is important to Charles. He's a grown man, and it makes him happy."

After looking back and forth between Charles and his wife, Pop finally nodded. "Yeah, you're right, Lori." He looked Charles in the eye. "You are a much better man than we raised you to be, and that's even more proof that the Lord is active in our lives."

Charles didn't want to take anything away from his parents, but he knew Pop was right. "The best thing you ever did for me was lead me to Christ."

Tears sprang to Mom's eyes so Charles decided to change the subject. He'd changed quite a bit lately, but since Mom rarely cried, his gut clenched.

"Where do you think I should take Ruthie for dinner?" he asked.

Pop thought for a moment before replying, "Why don't you ask her where she wants to go?"

"I don't know if she's been many places outside of Pinecraft."

"He's right, Jonathan," Mom said. "Let me give this some thought. In the meantime, you can ask Ruthie what some of her favorite foods are. That should help narrow the list."

When Sunday arrived, Ruthie was out of sorts. She'd applied for the job at Fresh's Yogurt Shop and gotten it. Mr. Fresh told her she'd start the following Monday, helping set up before their grand opening. The very thought of it sent her into panic mode.

"Why aren't you ready yet?" Mother asked as she stood at Ruthie's bedroom door. "We need to leave in five minutes."

"I can't get the kapp on right." Ruthie felt as though her hands had become detached from her arms as they shook.

"Here, let me help you." Mother walked right up to her, spun her around, and adjusted the kapp in a matter of seconds. "There you go. All your hair is in place, and your kapp is just right."

"Thanks." Ruthie looked down at the floor to avoid her Mother's gaze.

"Ruthie, stop worrying about tomorrow. You'll do just fine."

"I'm not so sure," Ruthie said. "You know how I can be when I'm nervous." She pointed to her kapp. "Even in the privacy of my own room, my hands are shaking. Can you imagine how embarrassing it'll be if I'm like this tomorrow?"

"Perhaps it won't be so embarrassing if you stop thinking about people looking at you. Consider yourself the Lord's servant and serve the frozen yogurt for Him."

Mother always did have a better perspective than she had. "Ya. You're right."

"You've always worried about offending people or doing something others don't approve of. The only thing you need to concern yourself with at this stage in your life, Ruthie, is following His calling." She backed toward the door. "Now take a deep breath, say a prayer, and meet your papa and me outside."

After Mother left, Ruthie did exactly as she said. When she finished her heartfelt but brief prayer, she felt much better. Her nerves hadn't completely calmed, but she felt more anchored.

The instant she arrived on the church lawn, she spotted Charles and his parents. Charles grinned at her and mouthed that he wanted to see her after church. She nodded.

Ruthie had to force herself not to let her mind stray throughout the service. She stared at the pastor during the sermon and tried to absorb what he said.

Afterward she followed Mother toward the door. Charles stood outside waiting. Her pulse quickened as she stepped closer to him.

"Good news!" he said, his face lit up.

Ruthie couldn't help but smile at the obvious joy he exuded.."Tell me. I'm ready to hear good news."

"If you'll accept, I'm taking you to the Ringling Museum of Art and out to dinner afterward. The only thing I need to know is what kinds of food you like or don't like."

"We can always go to Penner's," Ruthie said. "They have a wide variety."

Charles looked disappointed at first, but he quickly recovered. "If that's where you want to go, I'll take you there, but I thought…well, maybe… I don't know. How about we go somewhere different?"

"I haven't been to all that many places," she admitted. "So it's hard for me to suggest a place."

"Do you like seafood?"

"Ya. I like fish and crab cakes."

"Then I bet you'll like lobster. I know the perfect place."

Ruthie had never tasted lobster, but she knew it was pricy. "Isn't lobster awful expensive?"

Charles pursed his lips and nodded. "It can be but this is a special occasion, and I really want to treat you to something you'll always remember."

Ruthie didn't need lobster to remember being with

Charles, but he seemed so excited she didn't want to poke a hole in his joy. Instead she said, "We can go wherever you want to take me."

"Perfect!" He shifted his weight from one foot to the other. "Mom and Pop are waiting for me. Your birthday's on Friday, right?"

She nodded. "Ya, but if that's not a good night for you—"

"I don't want to interfere with your family's plans."

"My parents won't mind celebrating on a different day."

She was delighted to see him smile. "If your dad will let you off early, I can pick you up at two thirty. Abe has already given me the afternoon off."

"Um…well, I'm starting a new job."

"I heard. Mr. Fresh told me you start tomorrow, but the shop doesn't open for another week. He said you don't have to work on Friday afternoon either."

Ruthie wasn't sure how she felt about everyone making arrangements without consulting her, but this wasn't the time to bring it up. "Okay, then we can go at two thirty on Friday."

As soon as Charles left with his parents, Ruthie joined hers. Mother was the first to speak up.

"Did I hear Charles ask you out on your birthday?"

Ruthie nodded. "He's taking me to the Ringling Museum of Art and out for dinner afterward."

"Where is he taking you for dinner?"

"Someplace that has lobster."

Papa laughed. "In other words, someplace fancy."

"Have you ever had lobster before?" Ruthie asked.

"Once," Papa said as he closed his eyes and rubbed his belly. "It was absolutely delightful. It's one of those foods you can't get enough of."

Mother tilted her head back and laughed out loud. "Samuel, I haven't met a food yet that you can get enough of."

He grinned. "I do like to eat."

"You sure do," Mother said before turning her attention back to Ruthie. "I've never had lobster, but I've heard it tastes sort of like crab, only better."

"Then I'm sure I'll like it." Ruthie decided to change the subject. "I have to be at Fresh's first thing tomorrow morning. Mr. Fresh wants all the workers to help him set up, and he says we'll need to learn how to use the machines."

Mother cast a concerned glance at Papa. "Our Ruthie has never operated machines before. What if she doesn't like that job?"

Papa tightened his jaw. "I didn't think about that. Remember that you don't have to work there forever. I just want you to have the experience of working for someone outside the family."

Ruthie didn't bring up the fact that she was just as concerned about how Rosemary would cope in the souvenir shop as she was about herself working at a job she didn't like. Papa appeared deep in thought, so perhaps he was thinking the same thing.

Chapter Ten

Some of the men from the church had volunteered to come over and fix the Polks' house up to make it more attractive to potential buyers. All week the house was filled with workers painting and making small repairs. They painted the outside of the house, and they prepped the inside to be painted the following week. Abe had brought over a couple of fruit trees that would bear fruit in another year or two so they could add that to the listing, which the realtor said would help attract buyers.

Mom went straight home from work on Friday so Charles could have the car for his date. He tried to explain that Ruthie would be just fine riding the bus, but Mom reminded him they'd be getting rid of their car soon and this would probably be one of the last times he'd be able to use it. They'd decided to rent a house in or close to the Mennonite and Amish community of Pinecraft as soon as their house sold.

Charles came home from the farm before lunch.

The men were still at the house working, and some of the women had come by bus with food. Mrs. Penner invited Charles to join them, so he did.

"The men have a meeting at the church this afternoon so they will likely leave early but come back to finish their work," Mrs. Penner said.

"We appreciate everything."

Mrs. Penner's eyes twinkled with a knowing look. "I hear you're taking our Ruthie on a date this afternoon," she whispered.

"Yes," he replied. "She said she's always wanted to go to an art gallery, so I figured I'd take her to the Ringling Museum of Art."

"That is the best one," she said. "When Mary first came to live with us, we took her there, hoping she'd find some joy here." Mrs. Penner shook her head. "But unfortunately it didn't work. She was always quiet and kept to herself until Abe came along. We prayed for something, and the Lord delivered Abe."

Charles hadn't known that about Mary. "Abe and Mary seem very happy now."

"Ya," Mrs. Penner agreed. "Mary has turned into a joyful young woman with a sunny disposition. We never thought that would happen."

"I guess I still have quite a bit to learn about the people in the church," Charles said. "I used to assume everyone was happy all the time."

"Neh, not always." Mrs. Penner placed her hand on his arm and looked him in the eye. "Remember that even Mennonites have troubles. We need the Lord as much as anyone."

A comfortable silence fell between them before Charles nodded. "Thank you for reminding me."

"Ya." She let out a deep sigh. "We have problems but we handle them differently from outsiders. Before we make any decisions, we are called to first turn to the Lord for direction. Only then should we act, and when we act, it is never in anger...or at least it shouldn't be." She chuckled as though she thought of a private joke. "But trust me when I tell you we still feel anger."

After Mrs. Penner left him to help serve food to the other men, Charles reflected on all the things she'd told him. Now that he thought about it, he could see some of the anger that brewed beneath the surface in some people who didn't want to give his family a chance. He looked around at the dozen and a half people working on his family home and knew that those people weren't among those who resisted allowing the Polks into the church fold. These were the folks who took Mom, Pop, and himself at their word and accepted them for who they were right now rather than who they were in the past.

Charles bowed his head, thanked the Lord for all He'd done to take his family to this Christ-centered church, and prayed for guidance and direction on all their future decisions. When he opened his eyes, he saw Mrs. Penner watching him. She smiled and quickly turned back to what she'd been doing while warmth and a sense of joy came over Charles.

After a busy morning, Mrs. Penner shooed him

away. "You have something very important to do this afternoon. Go on inside and get cleaned up."

Ruthie paced as she waited for Charles. Since she'd been given the day off at Fresh's, she went to the souvenir store and offered to help, but Papa told her he didn't need her. Rosemary was holed up in the office, which didn't surprise Ruthie. Although Papa hadn't verbally expressed his dissatisfaction with his new employee, Ruthie could tell by the way he averted all discussion of Rosemary.

"You have a big date this afternoon, so go home and get yourself ready," Papa said.

"There isn't much to do. I've already bathed."

Papa leaned toward her and lowered his voice. "I'm not talking about the outside. Go home and spend some quiet time with the Lord. You should always seek guidance when you are considering a relationship with a man."

She met his firm gaze and nodded. "Okay."

"Your mother wants the family to celebrate your birthday tomorrow night, so start thinking about what you want for supper."

Ruthie smiled. "She already knows."

"Roast beef hash?"

"Is there anything better?" she asked.

"You are a very unusual young woman," he said. "Almost too easy to please sometimes."

Ruthie finally left the store and went home. She was relieved that Mother wasn't there because her nerves were on edge, and talking only made her condition worse.

As the time slowly passed and the time for Charles to arrive drew closer, she felt as though she might get sick. Papa's words about spending quiet time with the Lord rang in her head, so she closed her eyes and prayed for her nerves to settle.

At two twenty-five, she peeked out the front window and saw Charles sitting in his car parked at the curb. She inhaled deeply, slowly let the air out of her lungs, and opened the front door. He looked up and smiled. Her belly did one of its drop-roll motions, but she managed to smile back at him.

Charles got out of the car and helped her into the passenger seat before getting into his side of the car. "Mom and Pop wanted us to enjoy the car while we still have it."

"You're getting rid of it?" She studied his face, half expecting to see regret, but he seemed perfectly fine.

"Yeah. After hanging out with people from your church, we see how unnecessary it is."

"Will you miss it?"

"Absolutely, but once we get used to not having it, I'm sure we'll be just fine. Even having one car was an adjustment, but now that I look back, I realize it was insane to have three cars. We justified it by saying we were scattered in three different directions, and it wasn't always convenient to have to take a bus or catch a ride with someone else."

Ruthie didn't know about such things. "I've always had to ride buses, and I've never found it inconvenient."

"Oh, I'm with you on that. We didn't realize how much money we actually spent on the cars until we didn't have two of them." He held up one hand and used his fingers to count. "First, there's the cost of buying the car. Second, you have to put gas in it and change the oil. Then you have to maintain it, which can be quite costly. After you add the price of insurance, you're talking some major bucks."

Ruthie nodded. "That sounds like a lot of money."

"Even though it's not cheap to hire a driver, we're still coming out ahead." When they stopped at a red light, he turned to her. "Let's not talk about money today. This day is all about you and your birthday. It's your twentieth, right?"

"Ya." Ruthie never liked all the focus and attention to be on her, but she appreciated Charles's interest. "I find it hard to believe that I'm this old."

"Turning twenty-one did that to me." He slowed the car and took a turn before speeding back up. Ruthie watched the road as he maneuvered the car on the busy Sarasota streets, amazed that he seemed to instinctively know what to do. "So how's the new job?"

"Different. We haven't officially opened yet, which is good because I have so much to learn. I have to admit I'm nervous about messing up."

"I bet. At least you'll be dishing out something good."

The sound of sirens blared in the distance. Ruthie heard them but only gave them a brief thought.

Charles pointed up ahead. "We're here." They pulled into a parking lot and found a spot not far from the entrance. "I hope you enjoy this place as much as I have."

Ruthie accepted Charles's hand as he led her toward the main entrance. As they strolled through the museum, she was spellbound by the sculptures and fountains.

Charles pointed out some things he was familiar with. "That's the *Fountain of Tortoises*, a replica of one in Rome," he explained.

"Rome," she repeated softly. "That is like another world."

"It is," Charles agreed as he tugged her toward a room with a special exhibition. "Some of the art is permanent, but this will only be here another week."

Ruthie remained captivated by everything she saw. "I've never seen anything like it."

"Same here," he replied.

They walked through the museum and stopped at whatever interested her. Charles knew more than she thought he would about art, but what he didn't know, he enjoyed reading on the plaques next to the exhibits.

Finally he glanced at his watch. "We have another fifteen minutes before they close. If I'd known you'd enjoy it this much, I would have suggested coming earlier."

"Oh, no, we've been here two hours, and I've seen as much as I can handle in one day. It's all so beautiful and...different."

Charles stopped, turned her around to face him, and gazed down into her eyes. "Just like you, Ruthie."

In spite of her cheeks blazing, she couldn't budge. Having Charles so close and giving her such an intimate look had rendered her incapable of moving. She felt as though they were the only living creatures in the world until she heard a man clearing his throat behind her.

"Sorry to interrupt, folks, but we're closing in a few minutes."

Charles licked his lips and nodded. "We were just leaving."

As they stepped outside, Charles thought about what had just happened. He'd almost kissed Ruthie. What would she have done? Before being involved with the Mennonite church, he wouldn't have had to worry about it, but he didn't know if he was allowed to show affection, and if he did, if it would be okay to kiss her in public.

Ruthie was being awfully quiet, which had him worried. "What are you thinking?" he asked.

She shrugged but didn't answer. He opened her door and helped her into the car. As he walked around to his side, he tried to gather his thoughts enough to discuss what had just happened, but his mind had been rendered incapable of rational thinking.

So he decided to just come out and share with Ruthie the first thing that popped into his head. He took her hand and looked her in the eye. "I wanted to kiss you, Ruthie."

She blinked but still didn't utter a word.

"Would that have been okay?" he asked. "I mean, I've never dated a Mennonite girl before... Well, I haven't dated much at all, and...well, I..." He didn't know what to say, and now he feared he might totally blow any chance at all of Ruthie liking him.

Ruthie looked as perplexed as he was. "I'm not sure."

"Do Mennonites...well, do they kiss?"

"Of course we do." Her lips quivered into a smile. "But I've never...well, I haven't kissed anyone before."

Her simple admission drove his attraction to her through the roof. If he managed to get the nerve to kiss her tonight, he'd be her first.

Instead of pursuing this line of conversation, Charles decided to change the subject. "Ready for some lobster?"

She nodded. "Papa seems to think I'll like it."

He sure hoped she did. Fortunately, some of his old video games and gaming systems had brought in quite a bit of money. Mom and Pop had been shocked when he gave them several hundred dollars in cash and said he still had plenty to take Ruthie on their date. Mom actually started to cry. He forced himself back to the moment.

"I think you will, too. Lobster is one of my favorite foods."

"What else do you like?" she asked.

All the way to the restaurant, they discussed their favorite foods. He noticed that most of the items she named were simple dishes that could be found in most homestyle restaurants. Mom had never been a great cook, but he'd eaten enough meals out to know a good meat loaf when he tasted it.

They'd barely reached the restaurant parking lot when his cell phone rang. He lifted it to see who was calling, and when he saw it was Pop, he answered.

"Are you in a position to talk?" Pop asked with a gravelly voice.

"Yes," Charles said as he glanced at Ruthie, who sat looking straight ahead. "We just got to the restaurant. What's up?"

"Um… I hate to do this to you, but you might want to take Ruthie home now."

Adrenaline shot through Charles's veins. "Why? Did something happen?"

"Yes." Pop coughed.

"Is it Mom?"

"No, it's the house." He coughed again. "We had a fire. Someone tried to call you, but you must have turned off your phone."

"I left it in the car when we went into the art museum."

"It doesn't really matter because there was nothing you could do. Now we need you here."

"So tell me what happened."

Charles glanced at Ruthie as Pop explained that the house had been consumed by fire and nothing was salvageable. As he tensed, he noticed the concern on Ruthie's face.

"After you take Ruthie home, come on over to Penner's," Pop advised. "We have some decisions to make."

He punched the Off button and put the phone down on the console. Ruthie laid her hand on top of his. "What's wrong, Charles?"

"My family's house burned down. We lost...everything."

She gasped. "I am so sorry."

Charles looked at her and saw that she was sincere. "I hate to do this to you on your birthday, Ruthie, but I need to take you home now. My parents really need me."

"Of course," she said. "You don't have to apologize. I would be disappointed if you didn't go to them."

He drove straight to Ruthie's house, where her parents stood on the front lawn. Mr. Kauffman came to the car window and leaned over. "We heard what happened. If you need us, don't hesitate to call."

Ruthie's mother looked Charles in the eye. "We waited here, in case you decided to take Ruthie home. Would you like us to go with you?"

"I appreciate the offer, but I think we'll be fine."

"We would like to help in any way we can."

After Charles thanked him, he headed for Penner's, praying all the way there. The restaurant was still open, but there weren't many cars in the lot.

Charles didn't waste a minute. He hopped out

of his car and took off for the front door that was opened for him before he got there. Mr. Penner gestured toward the corner. "Your parents are in the corner booth."

To Charles's surprise, the place was packed with people—most of them not eating. Immediately after he made his way to his parents' booth, Mr. Penner walked up with a pot of coffee, and without asking if they wanted any, poured a cup for all three members of the Polk family.

Pop looked exhausted but resolved. Mom, on the other hand, appeared distraught. "Everything I owned was in the house. I don't think there's anything left."

She shuddered but relaxed when Pop put his arm around her. "Everything that matters is right here. No one was hurt." Charles was numb and had a difficult time wrapping his mind around the whole situation, so he didn't say anything.

Some of the people standing nearby discussed who was going to do what to help them.

Mr. Penner placed the coffeepot on the table and sat down next to Charles. "Most of us live in small houses, so we don't have room for your whole family. That's why you're staying with my wife and me, and your parents will stay with the Yoders."

Charles glanced at Pop, who nodded. "What about clothes?" Charles asked.

Mr. Penner spoke up. "Some people from church have already brought some things over to the house—clothes and other personal items. They should do for the time being. My wife is putting your things away right now."

When Charles looked back at Mom, he tried to picture her wearing the clothing from other Mennonite women. It was hard to imagine, but she didn't have much choice at the moment. Then he remembered the money he'd planned to spend on Ruthie's dinner.

"I still have a few bucks," he said. "We can go shopping if you want."

Mom shook her head. "No, keep that money for now. We might need it later." Then she turned to Mr. Penner. "Would you mind if I had my son drive me to the Yoders' house now? I'm tired."

Charles stood. "I'll come right back after I drop her off." People in the restaurant moved aside to make a path for Charles and his mom. Pop stayed behind.

Once they were in the car, Charles looked over at Mom as he turned the key in the ignition. "Any idea what happened?" She leaned back against the headrest and closed her eyes.

"No idea whatsoever."

"I'm glad no one was home." Charles shuddered to think about the disaster that could have been much worse.

"Oh, I didn't say I wasn't home. In fact, I was in the kitchen when I heard some popping sounds in the back of the house."

Charles stopped the car before pulling out onto the road. He turned to Mom. "What did you do?"

"I ran toward the sound, but by the time I got there, the whole bedroom area was engulfed in flames. So I did what any normal person would do. I ran out of the house screaming." She opened her eyes and offered a hint of a smile, but it quickly faded. "I can't remember ever being that scared before."

He lifted his foot off the brake and pulled out onto the road as he visualized Mom running from their burning house. "How long before the firemen arrived?"

"One of the neighbors must have called because I don't think I was outside more than ten minutes before they came. By then every room in the house was on fire."

When they arrived in front of the Yoders' house, Charles could see a roomful of people through the picture window. "Looks like you won't be alone."

Mom groaned. "I tried to talk your father into getting a hotel room for at least one night, but with everyone insisting we stay here, he didn't want to offend them."

"I'll go in with you." Charles made it to Mom's side of the car as quickly as he could so she wouldn't have to take a step without him by her side. She latched on to his arm and leaned into him as they walked up the sidewalk.

Mrs. Yoder opened the door, and they were quickly engulfed by the crowd that consisted of Jeremiah and Shelley Yoder, Jeremiah's parents, Shelley's parents, and a couple of other people from church whose names Charles couldn't remember. He could tell they'd been involved in a heated discussion by the way they acted when he and Mom walked in.

Jeremiah's mother quickly took Mom by the hand and led her away. "I'll show you where you can get cleaned up. I have some clothes out on the bed in the room you and your husband will be sleeping in."

After they left the group, Jeremiah walked up and put his hand on Charles's shoulder. "Tough situation," he said quietly. "Don't let anything anyone says bother you. Some people can't handle change, but they'll eventually come around."

Charles wasn't sure exactly what Jeremiah was talking about, but he had a pretty good idea. He nodded. "I'm too worried about Mom to let other people bother me."

"Don't worry too much. My parents will take good care of her."

Charles knew enough about Jeremiah's past of leaving the church and coming back to open arms from his family to believe his mom and dad would be welcome in the Yoder home. However, some of the other people in the room continued to scowl their disapproval as they chatted with Jeremiah's father.

"Is something going on that I need to know about?" Charles asked Jeremiah as softly as he could.

Jeremiah looked at Shelley, who nodded. "You better warn him," she whispered.

"Okay." Jeremiah tilted his head toward the kitchen then turned and headed in that direction. Charles followed. Once they were in there, he pulled out a chair and motioned for Charles to sit down, then he sat adjacent to him. "I'm sure you already know there's a small but vocal group that is trying to keep your family from joining. This might be all they need to reinforce their argument."

Charles's breath caught in his throat, so he coughed. "What?"

"It's not the general consensus of the church, Charles," Shelley said. "It's just a few who always fight change."

"Yeah, tell me about it," Jeremiah said as he raked his fingers through his hair. "When I came back, the same bunch told my family I'd never change."

"I've never been in a situation like this before," Charles admitted. "I have no idea what to do next. I guess I'll need to go to the house tomorrow and see if I can salvage anything."

Jeremiah shook his head. "No, you can't do that. The authorities have the area roped off." He cut a glance in Shelley's direction before leaning toward Charles. "You're not allowed to cross the tape until after they investigate."

Chapter Eleven

On Saturday, Abe sent word to Charles and his pop that he wanted them to take the day off and not even consider working on the farm. Charles drove over to the Yoders' and picked Pop up to take him to the charred remains of the house. Mom wanted to go, but Pop told her he'd rather she didn't, and Mrs. Yoder convinced her she should stay.

The acrid smell of smoke hung in the air so strongly, Charles could smell it when they were a block away. Pop's jaw tightened and he didn't say a word as they pulled up in front.

"It's hard to believe this is all that's left," Charles said, his voice hoarse with emotion. "Even the front porch roof is burned."

"You should see the backyard," Pop added. "Even the oak tree caught fire, and it'll need to be cut down."

Charles felt his throat constrict. Mom had planted the oak tree in Jennifer's honor the year she died.

Even though they'd planned to sell the house soon, they'd always assumed the tree would remain standing for decades. Mom had chosen an oak for longevity.

"One of the things the authorities are considering is arson," Pop said, his voice husky with emotion. "There's even a rumor that we might be responsible, since we were planning to sell in a tough market."

"I can't believe anyone would think we'd do something like this to our own place," Charles said as they walked around the perimeter of the yellow tape. "We have so much of our lives in there, and now most of it's gone."

Pop started to say something, but he stopped, squeezed his eyes shut, shook his head, and shuddered. Charles hadn't seen Pop like this in a very long time.

Some of the neighbors gawked, but no one came to see how they were doing. Charles thought about how with the three-car garage, he, Mom, and Pop pushed the remote on the garage door opener, pulled in, and closed it without getting to know any of the people on their street. There was never any reason to converse with the neighbors so they didn't.

"It's such a shame," Pop said. "I know that all the stuff we lost was unnecessary, but I wanted to be the one to get rid of it."

"Yes, I know, Pop." Charles flung his arm casually over Pop's shoulder, and together they walked back to the car. "What do we do now?"

"We have to find a more permanent place to live.

I appreciate the Yoders and Penners, but I don't want to impose on them any longer than we absolutely have to."

"I agree." Charles automatically went to the driver's side of the car and got in. Pop looked at him for a moment then opened the passenger door.

"Now that we don't have much left, why don't we just go ahead and sell the car?" Pop said.

"Are you sure?"

With only a brief hesitation, Pop gave a clipped nod. "Positive. Once we do that, we'll have nothing left to lose."

Charles couldn't argue that point, so he didn't even try. He'd gotten used to the idea of paring down, but he obviously never expected it to happen so abruptly.

All the way back to Pinecraft, they discussed what to do next and where they'd live. "The insurance company should cover the cost of a hotel room until we find a more permanent place," Pop said. "However, the claims adjuster said he needed an official report from the fire inspector to make sure it wasn't...um..."

"Arson?" Charles said.

Pop didn't answer right away, so Charles looked at him. He'd buried his face in his hands, and if his shaking shoulders were any indication, he was crying. Charles had only seen Pop cry once before, and that was the day after Jennifer's funeral. He'd managed to remain stoic for Mom until then.

He took his right hand off the steering wheel and

placed it on Pop's hand. "We'll get through this. I'm just glad Mom was able to get out before…well, before the whole house was consumed."

Pop removed his hands from his face to reveal blotchy cheeks and reddened eyes. "I can't stop thinking about what would have happened if I'd lost your mother."

Charles steeled himself against his own emotion to be strong for Pop. "Don't do this to yourself. Remember that the Lord is in control, and He chose to send her to safety. Now He wants us to pick ourselves up and do what we have to do to bring some normalcy back to our lives."

Pop cleared his throat and stared straight ahead for a few seconds. "Normal has changed for us."

"And that's what we wanted, right?"

"Yes." Pop closed his eyes again, only this time Charles could tell he was praying.

When they got to the Yoders' house, Mrs. Yoder ran outside, clearly eager to tell them something. Her eyes were lit up, and she was smiling, so Charles assumed the news was good.

"We found a small house for you to rent," she said. "It's a few blocks from here, and you will be within walking distance from almost anything you need."

"That's good, but I wonder how long it'll be before we can sign a lease. The insurance company needs to investigate before they give us any money."

Mrs. Yoder continued smiling. "You don't have to worry about that for now. We've already taken up a collection for the first month's expenses, so you can move right in."

Charles almost couldn't believe what he was hearing. Most of the people in this community had modest incomes, so their generosity had to come from deep in their hearts.

"We can't accept something like that," Pop said, although he was clearly as moved as Charles was. "It's too much."

Mrs. Yoder appeared crestfallen. "But this is something we do for our own. Don't let pride prevent you from accepting something the Lord wants us to do."

Charles stepped closer to his father. "Pop," he said softly, "I think we should accept."

"I've never... Well, no one has ever been that generous with us, first of all, and secondly, I've always been the one to do the giving," Pop admitted.

"That's all the more reason we should take what they're offering," Charles said. "I remember you saying how good it felt to give to others."

"Yeah, you're probably right, and my pride is too big for my own good." Pop swallowed hard, looked at Mrs. Yoder, and forced a smile. "Thank you."

Mrs. Yoder beamed with joy. "We love serving." A momentary cloud seemed to hover, and she added, "Most of us do, anyway."

The grand opening for Fresh's Yogurt Shop was on Saturday. Although Ruthie had mastered the machines and learned all about the ingredients so she could answer customers' questions, her nerves were frazzled.

Mother tried to calm her during breakfast. "You'll do just fine, Ruthie."

"What if I spill something or I dump a cone of yogurt onto someone?"

"I doubt that'll happen, but if it does, think of the worst thing that can happen." Mother had used this throughout Ruthie's life, but it still didn't ease her worries. "Now go on to the shop. We'll be praying for you."

As Ruthie left the house, her thoughts wandered to her date with Charles. She couldn't remember ever having such a wonderful time. The art museum was delightful, but even better was the feeling she got from simply being with Charles. He looked at her in a way that reminded her of how Papa looked at Mother, and the mere memory of it made her tingle. She felt safe and secure with Charles, even though they were in a place she'd never been. Ruthie had always had trouble adapting to new situations, but this one time was different. She sighed. Too bad the evening ended on such a sad note.

Ruthie had to walk past her family's souvenir store on the way to Fresh's, so she looked inside. Papa leaned against the counter talking to some men, and again, Rosemary was nowhere in sight. Acting on impulse, she pushed the door open and walked in. She had left the house a half hour early, so she had a little bit of time.

The men instantly stopped talking when they

heard the bell on the door. Papa looked up at her and tried to smile, but she could tell he was unhappy about something.

"Is everything okay, Ruthie?" Papa asked.

Ruthie nodded. "I'm on my way to work. We have our grand opening today."

Papa lifted a yogurt shop flyer from the counter and showed it to her. "I'll hand these to all our customers today. Business should be good—at least on your first day."

"I hope so," she said, although a part of her wanted no one to walk through the doors. "I just wanted to stop by and see you since you left before I got to the breakfast table." She leaned around the counter and looked toward the office, the door barely ajar. "Where's Rosemary?"

Papa pointed. "She stays in the office most of the day. I try to get her to come out, but she doesn't like being on the sales floor."

Ruthie understood how Rosemary felt, but she suspected there was something more to Rosemary's reluctance to help customers than shyness. "Does she come out when you have to leave?"

Papa nodded. "Ya. That's the only time she does though."

What Ruthie wanted more than anything at the moment was for Papa to tell her he needed her to come back and that it was all a mistake to send her to another job. But he didn't. She'd just have to put in her time, and hopefully he'd ask her to return when he was satisfied that she had enough experience away from the family business.

"Have a good day, Ruthie, and don't worry. You'll do just fine." Right before she got to the door, the men started talking again. When she overheard one of the men lambasting Papa for being so welcoming to the Polks, her stomach churned. She'd already heard about how a small handful of people from the church had gone to the authorities and claimed they had reason to believe the Polks had set the fire.

Anyone who spoke to Charles, Mr. Polk, or Mrs. Polk for any amount of time and got to know them would know that wasn't true. There was no doubt in Ruthie's mind that they were sincere in their quest to learn about the Lord. She'd also seen Charles's face when he heard about the fire, and based on how lost he suddenly appeared, he clearly had nothing to do with it.

Ruthie arrived at Fresh's at the same time as Zeke, another part-time worker, who was just as nervous as she was. "Part of me wants to be busy, but if we're too busy, I'm afraid I'll mess up," Zeke said. "But I suppose we should pray for a successful grand opening so we will be able to keep our jobs." The thought that she didn't want to keep this job flickered through her mind. Papa had tried to explain how she needed to get out and experience something besides their family business for a while, but she didn't get the point. Why change something that didn't need to be changed? She also had a bad feeling about Rosemary. She'd overheard Papa telling Mother last night that he always had to go over the books after Rosemary finished because she made so many mistakes. Ruthie had seen Rosemary in action, and she knew that Rosemary was competent in math. She didn't think Rosemary was sabotaging the shop, but her mind and heart obviously weren't in what she was doing.

Fortunately, early morning grand-opening business trickled in slowly and gradually increased over the course of the day. By midafternoon, they were packed, but Ruthie had gained enough confidence to handle the crowd. She even enjoyed helping customers decide what flavor to choose. Fortunately her boss encouraged them to offer samples.

Mr. Fresh staggered the workers' breaks, letting two of them take off fifteen minutes at a time. She was glad she had her break with Zeke. She'd known him since high school, when his family moved to Sarasota from Tennessee. Zeke's family was different from most of the other Mennonites in Pinecraft, and he had a way of making Ruthie laugh. As they sat in the back room talking, he cracked a few jokes then asked her if it was true that she was seeing the Polk boy. The way he asked was matter-of-fact rather than accusatory, so she didn't mind answering. And he always had a silly grin that she found endearing.

"He seems like a nice enough guy," Zeke said. "But I find it interesting he's trying to break in at a time in his life some of us are trying to get out."

Ruthie tilted her head in confusion. "Break in?"

"Ya, break in to the simple life. I've always wondered what it would be like to be out there in the world."

"That's what rumspringa is for," she said.

"My parents never went for that, and I didn't want to upset them since my father has a bad heart." He dropped his crooked grin as he reflected. "I don't recall you having rumspringa either."

"I never had the desire," Ruthie said. "We better get back to work so the others can have a rest."

Her shift was supposed to end at three, but Mr. Fresh asked her to stick around another hour if she didn't have any other commitments. "You're doing such a good job, Ruthie. The customers like you."

He couldn't have said anything to make her happier. Her last hour on the job flew by.

Mr. Fresh approached her with a wide smile as she took off her apron. "You did a wonderful job, Ruthie, and I hope you work here for a very long time."

She smiled back. "Thank you, Mr. Fresh. I did the best I could."

"Customers appreciate your quiet demeanor. You're not pushy and they trust you."

That small amount of flattery brightened her day. She hung up her apron and started her walk home. As she drew near her family's store, she slowed down a bit but decided not to stop. Papa was inside talking to a customer, and she was pretty sure she could see the light on in the office at the back of the store, meaning Rosemary was still there. Papa never left lights on that he wasn't using.

Mother glanced up from weeding the front flowerbed when she got home. "Oh, hi, Ruthie. How was your first day on the job?"

Ruthie stopped and talked about the grand opening and how the crowd had been steady. Mother seemed pleased as she went back to her weeding. Ruthie went inside to wash the stickiness off her hands, arms, and face from the frozen yogurt that had splashed on her.

She still hadn't heard anything about the Polks' house. Mother might know something, so she decided to ask her.

Charles drove his pop to Penner's where they picked up Mom. Mr. Penner had told her she didn't need to come to work, but she said she needed something to get her mind off the fire. She came out to the car looking haggard. "I take it you had a rough day," Pop said.

She closed her eyes and leaned back against the backseat. "I don't know why I thought working would help me get my mind off all we're going through. Seems like everyone who came in today— at least the locals—asked what we planned to do."

Pop glanced at Charles. "Tell you what. I'll take you back to the Yoders', and Charles and I will go look at the house we're about to rent."

Mom's eyes opened as she bolted upright. "What?"

"The people from the church found us a house to rent, and they're getting it ready for us. I'm surprised no one told you."

Mom rubbed her forehead. "They might have, but the way I've been all day, it wouldn't have registered unless someone came right out and handed me a set of house keys. Tell me about it."

"All we know is that some of the people from the church found us a house, and they're getting it ready for us to move into."

"Did you get the insurance money yet?"

"No, not yet," Pop said. He explained how generous some of the families were by paying all the house-related expenses for the first month. "I plan to pay them back, of course, but at least we won't have to worry about things for a few weeks."

Mom sat staring out the window in a daze as Pop told her that the fire marshal had promised to expedite the investigation so they could deal with the insurance company and move on with their lives. "What if they find something suspicious?" she asked. "Will we have to prove our innocence?"

"Don't worry so much, Lori," Pop said. "Let's continue to pray about it and trust that the Lord will protect us."

"I don't want to go back to the Yoders' now," Mom said. "I'd rather go with you and Charles."

Charles made a quick decision to do something he'd been wanting to do all day. "Tell you what. The two of you can go to the house, and I'll visit Ruthie. I'd like to see how her new job went."

Mom and Pop agreed, so he drove straight to the new frozen yogurt shop, where he got out so Pop could take over at the wheel. After Mom got in the front passenger seat, he closed the door and waved as they pulled away from the curb. Then he went inside to see Ruthie at her new job. But she wasn't there. Frustration welled in his chest. Seeing Ruthie could make all his worries seem less...well, less worrisome.

"She's not on duty now," Mr. Fresh said. "Would you like to try one of our delicious flavors? We're giving samples."

"I'd like to later," Charles replied. "But right now I want to see Ruthie."

"Come back when you have time. And bring your parents. I'm sure a little frozen yogurt will help cheer them up."

Charles had to pass the Kauffman family's souvenir shop on the way to their house, so he slowed down and glanced in the window. Mr. Kauffman was talking to Rosemary, who hung her head and occasionally nodded. It didn't appear to be a friendly conversation, so he quickened his pace so they wouldn't see him.

A few minutes later he arrived at Ruthie's front door. He was about to knock, but Mrs. Kauffman flung open the door before he had time to lift his hand.

"I'm so happy to see you, Charles," she said. "Come on in and join us for some coffee cake."

Between dealing with the house fire and wanting to see Ruthie, Charles still had so much on his mind he hadn't thought about food much. The mere mention of coffee cake sent his stomach rumbling as he followed Mrs. Kauffman to the kitchen. She turned and smiled.

"Sounds like you could use a good meal. Why don't I make you a sandwich?"

"I don't want you to go to any trouble," he said.

"Oh, it's no trouble at all. In fact, I enjoy feeding people." She walked into the kitchen and motioned toward the table, where Ruthie sat. "Have a seat and I'll bring your sandwich in a minute."

His pulse quickened as he saw Ruthie. "So how was your first day on the new job?"

Ruthie shrugged. "Okay I guess but busy."

"That's a good thing, right?"

"Ya. I guess it is." Ruthie took a sip from the cup in front of her. "How are your parents?"

Before Charles had a chance to say a word, Mrs. Kauffman glanced over her shoulder. "Did you have a chance to see the house you'll be moving into yet? My husband took over some dishes and cups. They might not be as nice as you're used to, but they'll work until you can find something you like better."

"I haven't, but that's where Mom and Pop are now. That was such a nice thing for everyone to do for us."

Ruthie raised her eyebrows, giving him the impression she didn't know what they were talking about. But she didn't say anything. Instead she sat and waited.

"It's not too much when several families participate," Mrs. Kauffman said as she cut the sandwich and carried the plate over to the table, where she set it in front of Charles. "I hope you like ham."

The ham was good but even better was being with Ruthie. Charles felt an odd combination of excitement, warmth, and security when he was with her. No matter what else was going on, looking at her sweet face gave him the feeling that all was right in the world.

Mrs. Kauffman joined them at the table with her cup of coffee. "The Penners are stocking the pantry. We weren't sure what your family liked to eat, so they're putting a little bit of everything in there. The Yoders brought bedding, and the Burkholders' older son had some extra furniture he wasn't using." Charles listened in amazement as she rattled off all the things people had done for his family. They'd thought of everything. "I just hope we can repay all of you, but it'll be hard as generous as you are."

"The way to repay anyone is to live for the Lord," Mrs. Kauffman said. "That is what most of us are trying to do." She stood. "I think I'll leave you two alone for a little while. I'm sure you have some talking to do after last night."

Ruthie blushed as her mother smiled down at her. Charles wanted to reach out and touch her red cheek, but instead he clasped his hands together on top of the table.

Once Mrs. Kauffman left the kitchen, Charles leaned toward Ruthie. "I had a really nice time yesterday until we got the news."

"Me, too." She started to smile but caught herself. "I am so sorry about what happened to your house. Any idea what caused it yet?"

"Pop and I talked about it, and we can't come up with anything. We've always been so careful, so I can't imagine what happened. Mom was in the kitchen, but according to her, it didn't start there."

"I hope the authorities find the cause soon," Ruthie said.

As their gazes met, he felt unsteady even though he was sitting. The desire to leap toward her and plant a kiss on her little bowed lips nearly overwhelmed him, but he didn't want to startle her. Instead he took a deep breath, shuddering as he exhaled.

"Once all this fire business is settled, I would like to take you someplace nice."

She offered a shy smile. "That would be very nice."

"As soon as we get settled in our new place, we can make plans. Pop wants to sell the car, though, so we might have to take the bus or call for a ride."

Ruthie beamed. "You already know I don't mind riding the bus."

Chapter Twelve

After Charles left the house, Mother enlisted Ruthie's help in the kitchen. As they worked, she chatted about a variety of topics, from the souvenir store to Ruthie's new job.

"The Polks are taking this whole thing extremely well," Mother said. "I'm sure it's difficult, but with the prayers and community support, they can get through this."

"Ya." Ruthie didn't know what else to say, so she just bit her lip.

Mother stopped stirring and smiled at Ruthie. "You and Charles seem to like each other very much." She turned back to the pot on the stove but continued talking. "Did you know that your papa and I didn't know each other very well before we decided to get married?"

Ruthie abruptly turned to Mother. "I thought you lived on neighboring farms."

"We did but that was only after your father moved

in with his grandparents after his parents were killed in a horse and buggy accident."

Ruthie knew Papa's parents had died young and that he and his brothers moved in with his grandparents, but he was born in the same general area as Mother. "Didn't you know him before that?"

"Well," Mother began slowly, "I'd seen him, and I knew who he was, but he is quite a bit older than me. It wasn't until his older brother asked me on a date that he even noticed me."

Ruthie blinked in shock. "You dated Uncle Paul?"

Mother giggled. "No, of course not. I wasn't interested in Paul. In fact, after I turned him down, your papa came to see me to find out what was wrong with me. It didn't take long to realize he and I were more suited for each other."

"I had no idea," Ruthie said. Her parents rarely discussed their past, so she assumed they knew each other for a long time, courted, and got married when Mother was old enough. "Uncle Paul is such a sweet man, but I can't see you and him...together."

"Ya, he is very sweet, and fortunately there were no hard feelings when your papa told him he wanted to court me."

"How long did you date Papa before you agreed to marry him?"

Mother gave her a sheepish grin. "Six weeks."

Ruthie was speechless. She couldn't imagine marrying someone after only dating for six weeks.

"I know you are in the early stages of your relationship with Charles, but I can see the sparks between you," Mother said. "While I realize love can happen quickly, I would like the two of you to wait a bit longer than your papa and I did. At least we shared similar backgrounds and faith. You and Charles don't have that."

"Mother! I haven't even thought about marrying Charles!" *At least not until now.* Ruthie placed the saltshaker back in the cabinet, pulled a fork from the drawer to turn the meat in the skillet, and turned her back so Mother couldn't see her face.

Before Mother had a chance to respond, Papa walked into the kitchen. "Rough day," he said. "I had to let Rosemary go."

Ruthie dropped the fork into the pan. "What are you going to do now?"

"I have no idea. Do you know someone who needs a job and is good with numbers?"

"I would like to come back to the store, Papa."

He shook his head. "No, you've got a job, and from what Rolf Fresh has said, you are very good with the customers." He smiled at her. "I'm proud of you, Ruthie."

"But—"

"I hear Lori Polk needs more hours, but Joseph Penner can't give them to her," Mother blurted. "How about hiring her part-time?"

Papa's eyebrows shot up, and he nodded. "Ya, that might be a good idea. Lori is apparently very good with numbers, and she seems to have a good head on her shoulders. I'll talk to her after they get settled in their new house." He chewed on his bottom lip for a moment as silence settled in the kitchen. Then he turned to Ruthie. "Since you're working part-time at Fresh's, I would like you to come in for a little while until we get Lori trained…that is, if she takes the job." He paused as he looked at Mother. "Is that okay with you, Esther?"

"Of course it is. I can handle things just fine around here."

As her parents chatted, Ruthie's thoughts went straight to Rosemary. She wondered what had happened—if Papa had another reason for letting her go. Something about Rosemary seemed suspicious.

Sunday morning, Charles woke up feeling out of sorts. He was still at the Penners', in Mary's old room. He sat up in bed and thought about all the things he and his parents needed to do, on top of working for Abe. Fortunately, Abe offered them extra time off when needed to get things in order. However, when Charles and Pop talked about it, they came to an agreement that they'd do as much as they could on their own time because there was so much work to be done on the farm.

The sound of Joseph Penner's booming voice rang through the tiny house. "Breakfast is ready for anyone who wants it."

Charles wasted no time getting out of bed, dressing, and straightening the room. He arrived in the kitchen ten minutes later.

Mr. Penner belted out a hearty laugh. "I knew

you'd be hungry. Have some biscuits and ham. If you want jam, there's plenty in the cupboard."

"Don't dillydally," Mrs. Penner said. "We like to get to church in time to help the pastor, and since you are our guest, we expect you to join us."

"Yes, of course." Charles nodded. "I would be honored." He saw the exchange of glances between Mr. and Mrs. Penner.

"Good boy," Mr. Penner said. "I suspect you want to see Ruthie, too. She's a sweet girl but awful quiet."

"Joseph," Mrs. Penner said in a warning tone. "Don't embarrass our guest."

Charles gobbled down a couple of ham and biscuit sandwiches, took a few sips of Mrs. Penner's notoriously strong coffee, and left to brush his teeth. He joined Mr. and Mrs. Penner on the front lawn for their weekly trek to the church.

As they rounded the corner, Charles caught sight of Ruthie pedaling her three-wheel bike, her parents right behind her on theirs. He grinned as she kept one hand on her skirt to keep it from billowing in the breeze.

Charles could tell when she saw him because her expression completely changed. His heart hammered as her eyes twinkled with recognition.

"The girl is smitten," Mr. Penner said, jolting Charles and reminding him he wasn't alone. "And apparently so are you."

Struck speechless, all Charles could do was smile. Mr. Penner laughed until Mrs. Penner shot him a look that quieted him down.

Throughout church, Charles cast glances in Ruthie's direction. He hoped Mr. Penner was right about Ruthie being smitten. He was certainly on the mark with Charles. The more he saw Ruthie, the more he wanted to be with her. Seeing the brightness of Ruthie's smile made the fire seem less disastrous.

Pop stood up after the service was over and pointed toward Mom. "I have the keys to the house now," he said. "Let's go get your mom and take a walk to the new place."

Ruthie stood by the church door. At first he thought she might be waiting for him, but when he saw her mother chatting nearby, he realized that was only wishful thinking.

As soon as Mom and Pop joined him, they headed toward the door. An expectant look crossed Ruthie's face, but it quickly faded as he walked past. *Maybe she was waiting for me.*

"Go talk to your girl," Pop said. "We can wait."

Charles spun around and headed straight for Ruthie, who now had her back to him. When he said her name, she turned to face him, and the instant they made eye contact, everything else around him blurred.

"I thought you left," she said softly. "Did you forget something?"

His mouth went dry as he nodded. "Yes. You."

She frowned in confusion. "Me?"

"I came back to see if you wanted to go look at the new rental house with my family."

"I... I, uh..."

Ruthie's mother turned around, touched his arm to get his attention, and smiled at him. "She would love to."

"But my bike—"

"We'll get it home. Don't worry about it," her mother told her before addressing Charles again. "And afterward why don't you and your parents come to our place for dinner?"

"I'll have to ask Mom and Pop."

"No you don't," Pop said from behind. "We'd love to come, if it isn't too much of an imposition."

"It's never an imposition," Mrs. Kauffman said. "Take your time. I'll have dinner waiting for you when you get there."

At first Ruthie felt awkward tagging along with the Polks to the house they were about to rent. However, Mrs. Polk chatted and made her feel at ease.

Ruthie wasn't sure if Mrs. Polk knew Papa was going to offer her a part-time job, so she didn't say anything. When they got to the house that had been set up for the Polks, Ruthie gasped. It was on the edge of Pinecraft so she rarely went by it, but last time she saw the place, she remembered weeds that had gotten so unruly they'd worked their way into the front window screens. Now the house appeared neat, tidy, and freshly painted. The lawn was mowed and the bushes trimmed. The screens had been replaced, and there was a Welcome sign on the front door.

Mrs. Polk's voice shook with emotion as she lifted

her hands to her face. "This is such a sweet little place, Jonathan. I love it."

Mr. Polk put his arm around his wife, and she buried her face in his shoulder. She and Charles quietly stood there, waiting to go inside.

Finally, Mr. Polk pulled a key from his pocket and led Mrs. Polk to the front door. After unlocking and opening it, he stood back to let everyone else in first. As they walked through the house, Ruthie recognized various pieces from other people's homes.

"I want to see the kitchen," Charles said.

His father winked at Ruthie. "Of course you do, son. That's always been the most important room in the house to you." He pointed in the opposite direction. "Your mother and I will take another look at the bedrooms, and we'll meet you in the kitchen in a few minutes."

Ruthie followed Charles to the back of the house, the most logical place for the kitchen. Once they found it, she studied Charles as he surveyed the small but functional room with a cooking station on one side and a wooden kitchen table that seated four on the other, divided by an island with a butcher-block counter. Two walls were covered with cabinets. A narrow pantry took up the small space beside the archway leading to the rest of the house. "Mom will love this," he said. "She always said she felt lost in the big kitchen in our old house."

"I hope you're right," Ruthie said. "Even if she doesn't like it, you'll have a place to stay until you figure out what to do next."

"I like it," Charles said as he leaned against the counter, folded his arms, and locked gazes with her. "After we get everything settled, I might think about striking out on my own."

Ruthie imagined herself striking out with him, but she quickly squelched her thoughts. She had no business harboring such ideas.

"I can't believe it," Mr. Polk said from the door. "The whole place has been furnished from one end to the other. We don't need to get anything to move in."

His wife ducked into the kitchen beside him. "Someone even put a few outfits in the closet."

Ruthie knew that Mrs. Penner had gotten some clothing donations from women who were the approximate size of Mrs. Polk, but she couldn't imagine Charles's mother wearing whatever she'd found. But Mrs. Polk was polite, and she didn't let her opinion be known.

"Yeah," Mr. Polk added. "There are a couple pairs of work pants and shirts in there, too." He paused. "Go look in your closet, son."

"C'mon, Ruthie," Charles said. "I want to check everything out."

Charles flipped the light on in the bathroom and pointed to the counter where a basket filled with toiletries lay. "Whoa. Someone thought of everything."

"You might not have all the things you're used to, but…" Ruthie's voice trailed off as she noticed Charles watching her. She shrugged. "It'll get you started."

"Looks like we have what we need." Charles

leaned against the wall and extended a hand toward Ruthie. "Come here, Ruthie."

She followed his command and took his hand in hers. To Ruthie's surprise, he pulled her all the way to his chest and wrapped his arms around her. She didn't know what to do, but she liked the way it felt being in his arms.

"Uncomfortable?" he asked.

Slowly she shook her head. He turned her around to face him then tucked his hand beneath her chin and tilted her face upward until their eyes met. She could feel her pulse in every inch of her body, from her head to her toes.

"Mind if I kiss you?"

Before she had a chance to respond, he'd lowered his head toward hers, and their lips touched—a feather-light touch at first then a more pressing kiss. The sound of voices drawing closer alerted them, so they pulled apart.

"Son..." Mr. Polk had just come into view of them standing in the doorway of the bathroom.

Mrs. Polk had caught up with her husband by now, and her eyes twinkled with acknowledgement. She grinned at Ruthie. "This is such a sweet little house. I think we'll be very happy here."

Ruthie was grateful that Charles's mother hadn't called them out on the embarrassing situation, but she was still humiliated by the fact that his parents saw what they did. Years ago a boy had tried to kiss her, but their teacher caught them. Embarrassed, he'd teased her about it on the playground later. Ruthie was all of twelve when she vowed never to kiss a boy again. Although she knew better than to hold herself to that promise, the old humiliation made her feel like a preteen again.

She cast a furtive glance in Charles's direction and noticed that he didn't seem to be the least bit embarrassed. If they'd been her parents, she would have wanted to crawl into a hole and not come out for a very long time. Not even Mother and Papa had public displays of affection, although she knew they loved each other deeply.

Chapter Thirteen

Charles heard footsteps coming through the house. He glanced at Pop. "Are we expecting anyone else?"

"No, but plenty of people know we're here, so it's probably someone from a welcoming committee," Pop said. "I'll go check and see who it is."

Ruthie still wouldn't look him in the eye since the kiss, and he wanted to give her time to recover. "I guess we're ready to move in."

"Charles," Pop said as he approached, "can you come outside for a minute?"

Mom started to follow, but Pop held up his hand. "Why don't you stay here with Ruthie?" He gave her a look unlike any Charles could remember.

When Charles got to the front door, he understood why. Mr. Krahn, Mr. Hostetler, and Mr. Atzinger were all on the front porch, glaring at him as though he'd committed a crime.

Charles tried not to assume anything, so he forced a smile and nodded. "Hi there, gentlemen. This is a very nice house the people from the church found for us."

"We didn't find it," Mr. Hostetler said, his voice gruff and unwelcoming. "That's why we stopped by. In case you haven't noticed, this community is made up of fine people who attend one of the Mennonite or Amish churches. We don't think outsiders would appreciate our way of life."

"We do," Pop said.

Mr. Hostetler glared at Pop as Mr. Krahn stepped forward to assume the lead. "You don't understand what he was saying. Pinecraft doesn't offer what people like you need. You are still outsiders to us."

Pop stepped forward with a finger lifted, but Charles took him by the arm and gently nudged him back. Charles spoke up. "I do understand what you're saying, but in case you haven't heard the news, we're seriously considering joining your church. Our needs have changed."

The men looked at each other and all nodded at the same time. "We don't feel that you are coming to our church for the right reasons."

Charles narrowed his eyes and looked directly at Mr. Krahn, who appeared to be the leader of the group. "Exactly what reasons do you think we'd attend your church if not for the right ones?"

"That is what we would like to know." Mr. Krahn folded his arms, and the other two men followed his lead. "Maybe it is for business purposes"—he turned to Mr. Hostetler before looking back at Charles—"or maybe you want to have our blessing to court one of our young women."

"No," Charles said softly as he placed his arm around Pop's shoulder. "You're mistaken. We've come to know the Lord through your church, and we've decided to embrace everything about it."

Charles could feel Pop's body tense even more as they waited for the men to say something else.

Finally, Mr. Atzinger spoke up. "I for one don't believe you, but I'm sure the truth will come out soon enough...after the fire marshal gives us the report."

"Ya, we have reason to believe—" Mr. Krahn started.

Pop yanked away from Charles, pointing to the street. "I would like for you to leave our property now."

"This isn't—"

Mr. Krahn tugged on Mr. Atzinger's arm. "Let's leave now."

Charles was angrier than he'd ever been in his entire life, but he had no desire to do anything but pray for the Lord's light to shine on what was right. Pop, on the other hand, seemed to have forgotten some of what he'd learned. "Let it go, Pop. We can't make them believe us."

In spite of the fact that Pop closed his eyes, apparently in prayer, Charles saw his father's fists clenched by his sides. If the majority of the church felt the way these men did, they wouldn't even want to be part of this church family. But most people were loving, accepting, and willing to help. The furnished rental house served as proof that there were enough kind people committed to encouraging the Polk family to make the effort worthwhile.

Pop opened his eyes and nodded. Charles could tell that he was still tense, but he'd done exactly what he'd been taught—to pray whenever sinful urges threatened.

Ruthie and Mrs. Polk had gone outside to see what was going on. While Mrs. Polk joined hands with her husband, Ruthie stood in stunned silence as the men from her church walked away without another word. She'd always known that Mr. Krahn was an angry man who resisted all change. But Mr. Hostetler and his wife had been friends of her family's until about a year ago, when Papa caught their nephew shoplifting from the souvenir store. They'd tried to defend the boy, but since Papa caught the boy walking out of the store with the merchandise stuffed under his coat, there wasn't much they could say. Even though Papa had decided not to call the police, the Hostetlers had pulled away and become tight with Mr. Krahn.

Charles tugged at Ruthie, pulling her from her thoughts. "I am so sorry they did this while you were here."

Ruthie cast her glance downward. "That was terrible. I don't know what to do."

"There isn't anything you can do," he said.

Perhaps there was, Ruthie thought. Maybe she should heed Mr. Hostetler's words and back away from Charles—at least for now—to give the Polks time to prove themselves.

She feared that she was making the Polk family's transition to the church more difficult than it needed to be, simply by being involved with Charles.

Ruthie saw Charles's parents cast a curious glance their way before Mrs. Polk took her husband by the hand and led him back into the house. She looked up at Charles and saw the concern on his face.

She took a step away from him. "I should go home now." Charles frowned. "I can take you home."

"That's not necessary." She swallowed hard as she continued putting more distance between herself and Charles. "Bye."

In order to break through the tug of her heart, she took off running as soon as she stepped onto the sidewalk. When she reached the edge of the block where she needed to turn toward home, she thought she heard someone calling her name, so she slowed down and glanced over her shoulder, expecting Charles to be right behind her. But he wasn't. He wasn't even in sight.

Ruthie gripped the Stop sign next to where she stood and bent over slightly while she caught her breath. She should have known better than to get involved with Charles—particularly at this time, with his family trying to join the church and with so many uncertainties that would cloud any relationship they could have.

The Polks' rental house was as far from her house as it could be in Pinecraft, so it took her a while to get home. She was glad, though, because it gave her time to regroup.

* * *

"Where's Ruthie?" Pop asked when Charles stepped back inside. Before Charles had a chance to answer, Pop gave Charles one of those concerned, narrow-eyed looks. "What just happened?"

Charles's mind still reeled from her abrupt departure. "I—I don't know. She told me she needed to go home, and after I offered to take her home, she took off running."

"Did you run after her?"

"No."

Pop shook his head. "You should have found out what she was thinking while it was still fresh. Now she'll wonder if you even care."

"What?"

"I've been married to your mother long enough to know that there are times when she needs me to show how much I care by working hard and digging for answers."

"I didn't think…" Charles cleared his throat. "I guess I just didn't think. Should I go after her now?"

Mom jumped into the conversation. "Your father is right, but now that you've let her go, why don't you give her a little time to think? That might be all she needs."

"But what if—"

"She's not going anywhere, son," Pop said. "If you don't see her sometime this coming week, you'll see her at church on Sunday. Maybe you can talk to her then."

Charles nodded and tried to consider Ruthie's perspective. He doubted she'd ever faced this kind of situation in her past, so giving her some space to mentally process what had just happened was probably a good idea.

"So what do we do now?" Charles asked. "Looks like the place is ready for us. Are we staying here tonight?"

"I think so," Pop said. "But it would be a good idea to go by and thank our generous hosts for putting us up and making this possible."

After they went to the Kauffmans', Yoders', and Penners' houses and expressed their appreciation, they went to their new home with baskets of food the women had prepared so they wouldn't have to cook for a while. Charles announced that he was hungry again, so Mom pointed to the baskets on the counter.

"Help yourself. You can help me put everything away after you're finished."

Charles filled a plate with baked chicken, mashed potatoes and gravy, green beans, a tomato and cucumber salad, and chocolate cream pie. Mom ate another piece of pie before patting her tummy and making her usual comment about needing to go on a diet. Pop laughed as he took her plate to the sink. "You look good to me no matter what, Lori. Don't worry if you put on an extra pound or two."

Before they went to bed, Pop called David to let him know they'd moved. "Yes, I know that," he said. "Abe gave me your new address. See you tomorrow."

Early the next morning, Charles and Pop waited for David on the front porch in the dark. Mom stepped out and informed them that she wanted to sell the car as soon as they finalized everything with the insurance company.

Charles looked at Pop, who nodded his agreement. "Yeah, I think that'll be a good idea. Then we can sell the vacant land and be done with it."

Mom leaned in for a kiss from each of her guys. "Have a good day at the farm," she said before darting back inside to get ready for her job at the restaurant.

Once she was inside, Pop shook his head. "Your mother seems much happier than she was before. I think she likes waiting on tables."

"I didn't see that coming," Charles said with a chuckle.

"Neither did I." Pop pointed to the road where a pair of headlights came toward them. "Looks like our ride is here."

Each day that passed when Ruthie didn't see Charles felt darker than the one before. "If I thought you would tell me, I'd ask if you were in love," Papa said.

Ruthie didn't respond. She'd just stopped by the shop to see if she could help, since Papa hadn't replaced Rosemary. He'd already prepared the bank deposit, so he handed the pouch to her to take to the bank.

"I've spoken to Joseph Penner about asking Lori Polk to work here a couple of hours in the afternoon," Papa said. "He said he'd send her over this afternoon."

Ruthie looked down at the floor. She had no doubt Mrs. Polk would do an excellent job. She had people skills as well as experience balancing numbers. If she agreed to work at Pinecraft Souvenirs, Papa wouldn't ever need Ruthie to return. Too much in her life was changing at once.

"Go on to the bank, Ruthie. I don't want you to be late for work."

Ruthie scurried out of the store and stopped by the bank on the way to the yogurt shop. The teller smiled as she took the pouch. "I'll have the transaction receipt waiting for your father tomorrow," she said. "Have a nice day."

With a nod, Ruthie went to work, feeling as though nothing was right in her world. She'd been displaced from her family business, and she had a job that was still uncomfortable for her, even though Mr. Fresh continued praising her. A group from the church had made it very clear that they were making it difficult for the Polks to become members because of her, and not wanting to stand in the way of what was really important to them, she'd had to pull away from Charles.

Even thinking about him made her stomach ache. Papa was right. She had fallen in love with Charles. Until now she never understood what a romantic relationship was all about. She loved the strange sensations she had from being with Charles, and he acted like he enjoyed being with her, too. But being apart from him was painful.

Ruthie wished she had someone to talk to—

someone who would understand what she was going through. She racked her brain trying to think of anyone who'd fallen in love with an outsider until she remembered how Shelley and Jeremiah had gotten together. He wasn't completely an outsider like Charles, but he'd left the church long enough to create controversy. Maybe she could talk to Shelley.

That would be difficult for Ruthie, though, because Shelley had as much confidence as Ruthie lacked. When Shelley wanted something, she didn't stop going after it. The more she thought about the similarities and differences between herself and Shelley, the more she realized confidence was the key.

Ruthie's shyness had prevented her from stepping out and doing what she really wanted to do. Until now she preferred the safety net of hiding in the family home and business. But everything had changed. She didn't have that safety net any longer. It was time to bust out and take charge of her own life. Papa had probably seen that, which was why he was pushing her outside her comfort zone.

Before she did anything though, she'd try to talk to Shelley. Since Mrs. Polk was still officially in training at Penner's, Shelley continued working there, so Ruthie knew where to find her. Maybe she'd run over to the restaurant during her break.

Mr. Fresh greeted her at the door, but the instant she walked in, he frowned. "Are you not feeling well today?" he asked.

"I'm okay."

"If you want, you can do the prep work for a little while…until you feel like facing customers."

Ruthie forced a smile. "I'm really fine."

"If you're sure…"

She nodded as she brushed past him to get her apron. Without another word, she took her place behind the counter and took the next customer's order. Although she still didn't feel 100 percent confident, she was getting better and less fearful of messing up each day.

The shop was so busy, time flew by until break time. She tossed her apron onto the counter and ran down to Penner's where Shelley stood by the coffee station, waiting for a pot to finish brewing. She glanced up and smiled at Ruthie.

"Hi there. Did you need a menu?"

"Not today," Ruthie said. "I just wanted to know if you could talk to me sometime soon."

Shelley frowned with concern. "Is there a problem?"

"Sort of, but I'm on break now, and I don't have time to discuss it."

"What time do you get off work today?" Shelley asked.

"Three."

Shelley glanced over at Mrs. Polk who was waiting on a table. "I'm supposed to work through cleanup after the lunch shift, but Mrs. Polk is doing so well, I think Mr. Penner will let me go early. I'm meeting Jeremiah at his parents' house after work. Why don't you stop by, and we can walk together?"

"Thanks!" Already Ruthie felt a load being lifted. She was glad Jeremiah's parents lived a block from her.

The rest of Ruthie's shift went by very slowly, so when Mr. Fresh said it was time to leave, she was ready. All the way to Penner's Restaurant, she prayed that Mr. Penner would let Shelley leave an hour early. To her delight, Shelley was outside waiting for her. However, as she got closer, she saw the sadness on Shelley's face.

"Did something happen?" Ruthie asked.

Shelley hesitated then nodded. "Ya. We just heard bad news about the Polks."

"What?" Ruthie couldn't have heard right.

"Mr. Hostetler came by after you were here and said he talked with one of the people at the fire department. They said it appeared that someone had started the fire intentionally. They found evidence of some accelerant chemicals that could have been used to start the fire."

"Did the authorities actually find something, or is this conjecture on Mr. Hostetler's part?" Ruthie asked as numbness crept over her entire body.

"That's what Mr. Penner asked. Mr. Hostetler reminded him that it is difficult to sell a house these days, and the Polks were struggling to keep up with their bills."

"But…" Ruthie didn't have any idea what to think, let alone say. All the questions she'd planned to ask Shelley were now irrelevant. Then she thought about the fact that Mrs. Polk still worked at Penner's.

Chapter Fourteen

"So what did you need to discuss?" Shelley asked. "Is Mrs. Polk still working at Penner's?"

Shelley nodded. "Mr. Penner said he didn't want to do anything drastic until he sees the final report, but I suspect he'll have to let her go. Oh, by the way, did you know that your father wanted her to come by and see him this afternoon?"

"Ya."

"I guess you better let your father know about the Polks."

Ruthie nodded. "I will."

"What else is on your mind, Ruthie? I'm sure you didn't want to talk to me about Mrs. Polk working at Penner's."

"It doesn't matter now," Ruthie said. "I think my problems have just taken care of themselves."

They walked in silence for a few seconds before Shelley spoke up. "So it's true, isn't it?"

"What's true?"

"You and Charles Polk have fallen in love."

Ruthie couldn't lie but this wasn't the right time to admit something she couldn't do anything about. So she didn't say anything.

"That's okay if you are, Ruthie. Granted, if Charles was responsible for the fire, you'll need to learn to get over him, but if he wasn't, the Lord will see a way to bring you together—that is, if it is His will."

"I don't know, Shelley. This whole situation has gotten so complicated. I don't think it's meant to be that way."

Shelley laughed out loud. "Trust me when I tell you that this isn't any more complicated than when Jeremiah and I fell in love."

"But you knew what to do."

Shelley stopped and turned to face Ruthie. "Is that what you think?"

"Ya. You always know what to do."

"Not at all. In fact, I had no idea what to do. Between my little brother pulling his disappearing act all the time, my mother's depression, and my father being at work most of the time, I thought there was no way I could fall in love with someone who'd left the church and been so...wild."

"But everything worked out for you and Jeremiah," Ruthie reminded her.

"Ya, and that was all the Lord's plan and His work. I didn't see how Jeremiah and I stood a chance for a very long time."

Ruthie found some comfort in Shelley's words,

but that still didn't negate the fact that the Polks were suspects in their own house fire.

"If I have any advice to give," Shelley continued, "it would be to continue praying and let the Lord lead the way. The truth will most likely come out, and once you have the facts, He'll show you what you need to do." She offered a comforting smile. "And I'll pray for you along the way."

Abe walked out to where Charles, Pop, and a couple of temporary workers were plowing a new section for some fall crops. Pop lifted a hand in greeting but continued working. Charles had to do a double take at Abe, whose expression didn't change. Normally he offered at least a hint of a smile.

"Jonathan and Charles, I would like to speak with the two of you for a few minutes."

"Sure thing, Abe," Pop said as he straightened and brushed the dirt off his hands. "When?"

"Now." Abe turned and walked back toward his house, leaving Charles and Pop to wonder what was going on.

One of the other workers said he'd take care of the equipment so they could follow Abe. All the way, Charles tried to figure out what could be so urgent.

Once they arrived at the picnic table beneath the shade tree, Abe gestured for them to sit. After they were in place on one side of the table, Abe sat down across from them.

"I just heard that there's some reason to believe the fire at your house was caused by arson."

Charles and Pop both gasped. "What?" Pop said. "Who would do something so terrible?"

Abe's temple pulsed, and he nodded. "According to Mr. Hostetler, you are the prime suspects. Some of the little explosions were from aerosol cans throughout the house and a case of craft finishing spray in the attic."

"Mom got a good deal on craft supplies, but she never used it all, so I put it up in the attic to get it out of the way. How can they think—"

"Ya, but that's not the biggest concern. Mr. Hostetler claims that the authorities are most concerned about the chemical accelerant you purchased the day before the fire. They found it in the bedroom where the fire started."

"Chemical accelerant?" A sick feeling washed over Charles. "Where does Mr. Hostetler get his information?"

"I am not certain, but I have heard he's been talking to the firemen. Unfortunately, they are merely speculating on limited information they've received."

There was no way he would have or could have started the fire. First of all, nothing like that ever crossed his mind. And secondly, he wasn't even home when it happened. Abe couldn't possibly believe they were guilty. "I was with Ruthie when the house burned," he said.

"True," Abe acknowledged, "but your mother was home." Pop tensed but he didn't move. Charles had no doubt his father was as confused and enraged as he was.

Abe stood. "I'm not saying I believe them. In fact, I don't. I just wanted to let you know what is going on so you aren't surprised when you go back into town this evening."

"Do...do you want us to continue working?" Charles asked.

"It is up to you. If you feel that you are capable of working after getting this news, please continue. If not, I will understand."

Charles turned to Pop who had buried his face in his hands. He wanted to wrap his arms around the man who'd raised him to always do the right thing and let him know that everything would be all right. But at this point, he wasn't sure about anything.

Charles looked back up at Abe. "Can you give us a few minutes alone?"

"Ya. Just come to the house and let me know what you decide."

After Abe was out of hearing range, Charles looked at Pop. "What do you want to do?"

Pop rubbed his neck and sighed. "If all we had to worry about was us, I'd say let's stay here. But your mother is in town by herself. No telling what she's having to deal with."

"Good point." Charles thought about it for a few seconds. "How about if I stay and you go be with Mom?"

A hint of a smile flickered on Pop's lips as he nodded. "Good thinking, son. I like that idea."

Together they went to Abe's house to let him know what they'd decided. "Abe, I can promise you that no one in our family did a thing to start that fire. I have no idea what the authorities found, but we didn't do it."

Abe held his gaze then looked at Charles before he nodded. "I believe you. Let's say a prayer together before we call David to come for you."

Shelley's talk helped Ruthie get through the remainder of the day. When Ruthie and her parents sat down to supper, Papa didn't waste any time talking about the Polks.

Papa had offered Mrs. Polk the job, in spite of the warnings from Mr. Krahn and Mr. Hostetler. "I don't believe she had anything to do with the fire," he said firmly when Mother questioned his judgment.

"But the authorities said—"

Papa's glare stopped Mother midsentence. "Mr. Hostetler is the one who said that, not the authorities. Jonathan came into the store this afternoon," Papa added. "He looked worried sick about his wife, and I can't blame him."

Mother shook her head and clucked her tongue. "This has to be difficult on the whole family. If they're found innocent, I can't imagine them wanting to continue attending our church."

Papa shook his head. "Don't forget the power of the Lord, Esther. He's in control, not us. If He wants them to stay with our church, they will."

Ruthie remained quiet, although she agreed with Mother. If she were in Charles's position, she would seriously consider running as far away from the accusers as she could.

"Remember that those doing the accusing are still in the minority. There doesn't appear to be conclusive proof that the Polks did anything wrong," Papa added. "Most of us still don't believe they're guilty."

Mother tilted her head and raised her eyebrows. "According to the sewing group, a lot of people are changing their minds now that there's some evidence."

Ruthie jumped at the sound Papa made. She'd never heard him growl like that before.

"Samuel!"

Papa exchanged a glance with Mother before turning to Ruthie. "I found out that Rosemary has been reporting back to her uncle, who has joined the group against the Polks. I don't understand how a girl raised in the Word can do something so deceptive. She didn't want to work for me, so she tried to use this tragedy to convince her uncle she should leave." He shook his head and lowered his gaze to the table before looking Ruthie directly in the eye. "Sorry, Ruthie, but this is so frustrating. I wish there was something I could do to make everything right."

That was one of the things Ruthie most admired about Papa: his sense of justice. He had a very strong sense of right and wrong, and the line between them was bold. Ruthie had all sorts of questions about Rosemary, but she knew how Papa was about letting things go.

"When does Lori start the new job?" Mother asked.

"Tomorrow," he said. "She's coming in immediately after she finishes her shift at Penner's."

Mother frowned. "I can't imagine wanting to work two jobs."

"She said she's thankful for the work," Papa said. "Her family needs the money to pay off some of their bills. That's one of the reasons I believe in their innocence. The Polks don't seem to mind hard work. In fact, Abe says Jonathan and Charles are very industrious, and they are an asset to his team of workers." He looked at Ruthie. "Do you have plans to see Charles soon?"

"Neh." Ruthie looked down. "I don't think I'll be seeing him anymore."

"Do you think they're guilty?" he challenged.

"No! I don't believe for one minute they're guilty, but if I continue seeing Charles, Mr. Krahn and the other men will never leave the Polks alone."

"That is not a good enough reason to stop seeing someone you love, Ruthie," he stated firmly. "That is, if they're innocent."

"Correction." Mother grinned and winked. "That is, if you love him."

Papa leaned back and folded his arms. "Ruthie, are you in love with Charles?"

Both of her parents watched her without blinking. Ruthie had never lied to them before, and she didn't plan to start now. She slowly nodded. "Ya, I believe I am." She cleared her throat. "Or at least I was."

Pop stayed in town the next day to talk with the fire marshal. Charles went to the farm with the understanding that he'd come home if needed. Mom went to her job at Penner's because she felt she was better off busy than trying to help when she didn't have any idea what she could do to help.

Throughout the morning, Charles glanced up toward Abe's house to see if there was any sign of news. When lunchtime rolled around and no one came to get him, he headed to his favorite spot under the shade tree. He'd barely opened his lunch bag when David's van came rolling up the sandy road.

Charles started to pull out his sandwich, but when he saw what appeared to be Ruthie sitting beside Pop, he paused. No, that had to be his imagination. What would Ruthie be doing here?

David pulled to a stop, but no one got out of the van right away. That was odd. Pop generally hopped right out so David could get to his next fare.

Charles put his lunch bag down, got up off the picnic bench, and walked toward the van. He was about twenty feet from the van when he saw that his eyes hadn't played tricks on him. Ruthie really was sitting next to Pop, and they were talking with David about something.

He paused for a moment until Ruthie turned and looked directly at him. His heart felt as though it would pound right out of his chest. Instead of waiting, he ran toward the van and yanked open the door.

"What are you doing here, Ruthie?"

Pop shook his head and chuckled. "Why are you talking to your girlfriend like that, son? After I got some good news, I went to tell her and her parents.

She wanted to see you, and who am I to stand in the way?" Charles noticed the joy on the faces of both Pop and Ruthie.

"But—"

"I spent the morning with the fire marshal, and we've been cleared of any wrongdoing. The chemicals they found were paint thinners used on the exterior of the house."

"Do the authorities know how the fire started?" Charles asked.

"Some faulty wiring that got out of control when sparks ignited the materials we used for painting," Pop said. "Now that they know we had nothing to do with it, the insurance company is going to come through and settle everything." He got out of the van and helped Ruthie out.

Ruthie smiled at Charles. "I am so glad that's all over with."

Charles wasn't sure what to do next, but Pop was right on top of the situation. "Don't let this girl get away, son. Make sure she knows how you feel." Pop gave him a gentle nudge with his elbow. "Do it now."

"Um… Ruthie, I like…no, I love you, and I'd like to spend the rest of my life with you."

"Whoa, son," Pop said with a chuckle. "That's not exactly what I was talking about. Slow down and wait until the timing is right…and you're alone."

"You said not to let her get away."

Pop didn't try to hide a goofy grin. "I did say that, didn't I?"

"See?" Charles heard David laughing in the background, but that didn't bother him. "And she went to all this trouble to come out here with you, so I'm not wasting another minute. I love Ruthie, and she's the girl I want to marry."

"Well…" Pop got David's attention and motioned to follow him to the tree. "Since I can't control my son's sense of urgency, why don't we go over there and give them some space?"

"You don't have to do that," Charles said. "I don't care if everyone in the world knows how I feel."

David was still laughing as he and Pop left him and Ruthie alone.

"Well?" Charles said as he turned back to face Ruthie whose face was flaming red. "Do you feel the same way?"

She looked down for a few seconds then slowly raised her gaze to meet his. He held his breath until she finally nodded. "Yes, Charles, I do feel the same way."

"Okay then." He sucked in a breath. "I guess I should have asked your father for your hand first, right?"

"Probably"—Ruthie gave him a shy grin—"but I think he'll understand."

Ruthie's nerves were a tangled mess as she rode back home in silence. Occasionally she caught David glancing at her in the rearview mirror, but once she looked at him, he turned his attention back to the road. After he pulled up in front of her house, he hopped out and ran around to open her door.

As soon as Ruthie's feet hit the ground, David

leaned over and whispered, "Congratulations. I'm glad Charles found such a sweet girl."

Ruthie felt her cheeks grow hot, but she didn't look away as she would have in the past. Instead she met his gaze and said, "Thank you."

Before entering her house, she stood facing the front door and inhaled the air that had started to cool down a bit. Charles said he would be here after he got home from work because he wanted to talk to her parents. She knew it would be difficult not to say anything to her parents, so she hoped Mother wasn't home.

The instant she walked inside, she heard Mother puttering around in the kitchen, so she went straight to her bedroom. Mother must have heard her because she was there in a matter of seconds.

One look at her, and Mother narrowed her eyes. "What's that funny look about, Ruthie?"

Ruthie just smiled.

Mother's eyebrows shot up. "I heard the news about the Polks' innocence. Your father and I are very happy."

"Ya. Me, too." Maybe Mother wouldn't guess the rest.

"I need your help with supper. Your papa will be home early tonight. He said we're having company for dessert."

Ruthie's heart thudded. Tonight wasn't a good time to have company. "Who?"

"The Polks, of course. We have a wedding to discuss." Mother smiled as she closed the distance between them and gave Ruthie a big hug.

"You know?"

"Of course I do." Mother chuckled as she captured a stray strand of Ruthie's hair and tucked it beneath her kapp. "I am so happy for you, Ruthie. Charles is a very sweet boy, and his family is so nice."

Ruthie couldn't keep the tears from falling. Mother dabbed at Ruthie's cheeks with her sleeve.

"Why don't you freshen up and change clothes before everyone arrives?"

Ruthie was in her room changing when she heard Papa walk in the front door, so she hurried in order to join her parents. Papa motioned for her to join them for a family discussion.

"I want you to know that the church is demanding a public apology from the troublemakers," he said.

"Have they apologized to the Polks yet?" Mother asked.

"Mr. Hostetler is over there right now, doing just that. I pray they find it in their hearts to forgive him."

"Even for us it would be difficult, after those terrible accusations," Mother said.

"What if the Polks can't accept their apology?" Ruthie asked.

Papa placed his hand on her shoulder. "Do not worry about what you cannot control, Ruthie. This is in the Lord's hands now. The church council is going to meet with all the families who tried to prevent the Polks from joining."

Charles was nervous as he and his parents took off on foot for the Kauffmans' house. Pop hadn't wasted any time letting Mom know, and Charles had spoken to Ruthie's father when Abe sent him home early. This would be the first time the two families would come together knowing they'd eventually all be part of one big family.

"Mr. Hostetler seemed very sorry," Mom said. "I feel bad that he and the others have to speak in front of the church about what they did wrong."

"I believe it's the right thing for the church to do." Pop smiled. "It reinforces my decision that we're doing the right thing." He turned to Charles. "You okay, son?"

Charles cleared his throat. "I'm very nervous."

"Relax, son," Pop said as they started up the walkway to the front door. "Everything will be just fine."

Before they got to the door, Mr. Kauffman flung it open and pulled Charles into a bear hug. "Welcome to the family, Charles." Then he turned to Mom and Pop with only slightly less enthusiastic hugs. "Esther and I are very happy."

Charles saw Ruthie appear at the front door, her sweet, smiling face lighting up the near darkness.

"Go on, son," Pop said as he nudged him toward the house. "She's waiting for you. Go make some memories."

Without wasting another second, Charles ran toward Ruthie and pulled her into his arms. He leaned down and whispered, "Okay if I give you a kiss?"

She nodded. As he kissed her, their parents let

out deep sighs, reflecting what Charles felt in his heart. He pulled away and looked into Ruthie's eyes.

"I love you," he whispered.

"I love you," she said without an ounce of reservation. Yes, this was a moment he'd never forget.

Epilogue

Ruthie stood in the churchyard with her brand new husband of half an hour, watching Mary and Abe take turns chasing after their toddler. Her heart overflowed with joy, love, and peace like she'd never felt before.

"That'll be us in a few years," Charles whispered.

She turned to face the man she loved and trusted with all her heart. "I certainly hope so."

As if on cue, Shelley approached and opened the blanket so Ruthie and Charles could get a better look at the bundle in her arms. Ruthie's heart did a little flip. "He smiled at me."

Shelley offered a beatific grin. "He senses your joy."

Ruthie sighed. She couldn't ever remember a time when she was this happy. She had a husband she adored, parents who loved her, in-laws who were happy to share their son with her, and friends who were a few steps ahead of her so she would have someone to ask questions when she and Charles started their own family.

"C'mon, Mary," Abe called from the edge of the lawn. "Grab Elizabeth and let's go. David will be here any minute." As their friends left the churchyard one by one, Ruthie and Charles hugged them and accepted their best wishes. They soon found themselves alone.

"Ready to go home now, my sweet wife?" Charles asked.

Ruthie's eyes misted as she nodded. "Yes, my loving husband. I am ready to go to *our* home."

* * * * *

WE HOPE YOU ENJOYED THIS BOOK FROM

LOVE INSPIRED

INSPIRATIONAL ROMANCE

Uplifting stories of faith, forgiveness and hope.

Fall in love with stories where faith helps guide you through life's challenges, and discover the promise of a new beginning.

6 NEW BOOKS AVAILABLE EVERY MONTH!

LIHALO2020

HARLEQUIN

Heartfelt or suspenseful, inspiring or passionate, Harlequin has your happily-ever-after.

With new books published every month, you are sure to find the satisfying escape you know you deserve.

Love Harlequin romance?

DISCOVER.

Be the first to find out about promotions, news and exclusive content!

f Facebook.com/HarlequinBooks

y Twitter.com/HarlequinBooks

○ Instagram.com/HarlequinBooks

P Pinterest.com/HarlequinBooks

ReaderService.com

EXPLORE.

Sign up for the Harlequin e-newsletter and download a free book from any series at **TryHarlequin.com**

CONNECT.

Join our Harlequin community to share your thoughts and connect with other romance readers!
Facebook.com/groups/HarlequinConnection

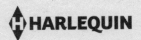